The Legend of Mistletoe Village

It is said that the month of December brings something very special to the sleepy New England countryside. Every year around Christmastime, a village appears where empty farmland stood. Certain selected people are drawn to this village for a reason unknown to them, and they stay for several days.

To the naked eye, it looks like your typical small town, with warm and friendly inhabitants inviting the visitors to join in their holiday festivities. But in the process, these visitors learn a great deal about themselves, and their lives are changed forever.

Unbeknownst to these people, something very strange happens to the little village of Mistletoe at midnight, December 26. The entire town shimmers into silvery shadows until it completely disappears, and the countryside is quiet and empty once more. The village residents wait quietly until the next tenth day of December arrives, when they can return to life and give another very precious gift—an understanding of what Christmas and love are all about.

Dear Reader,

As your typical kid, I believed in Santa Claus. I loved Christmas and the sparkle of bright lights, singing carols and participating in my school and church pageants. And I still remember the night I woke up and heard sleigh bells overhead but didn't dare get out of bed in case Santa was arriving rather than leaving!

To this day, I love going out and finding those special gifts for people, spending an evening wrapping them, decorating the house, addressing cards and having friends over while our dogs wear their special party collars and T-shirts so they can share in the fun. It's a great time, and Bob and I do our best to keep the feeling all year round.

In *No Room at the Inn,* I tried to convey the magic of an adult rediscovering the awed wonder of a child during the holiday season, whether by stumbling onto an object that holds a special holiday memory or by finding out that Christmas doesn't mean "bah, humbug." It means "peace on earth, goodwill toward *everyone!*"

May you and your family have a wonderful holiday season.

Linda

Linda Wisdom

Linda Randall Wisdom

NO ROOM AT THE INN

Harlequin Books

TORONTO • NEW YORK • LONDON
AMSTERDAM • PARIS • SYDNEY • HAMBURG
STOCKHOLM • ATHENS • TOKYO • MILAN
MADRID • WARSAW • BUDAPEST • AUCKLAND

To Mary Ellen O'Neill, who's suffered through so much with me and can still laugh without sounding hysterical!

ISBN 0-373-16515-3

NO ROOM AT THE INN

Copyright © 1993 by Linda Randall Wisdom.

Printed in U.S.A.

Prologue

December 9
Boston

"Quinn, I don't understand why you have all this hostility toward your mother. I think the real reason you're upset with her is because she and Nick want to spend the holidays in Barbados rather than here in town."

Quinn O'Hara gripped the receiver in one hand and crumpled the lacy bra in the other, wishing it was her mother's lovely swanlike neck instead.

"Alan, I really don't care to discuss my mother's holiday plans. I'm just glad she and Nick decided not to go to Jamaica. Especially with Dad and Mindy spending the holidays there. It wasn't a pretty sight the last time Mother ran into Dad with his wife of the moment." She rolled her eyes at the mental picture of her father's latest wife. She had to be a good ten years younger than Quinn and boasted a former career as a well-known stripper. Correction, exotic dancer. "Those two couples staying on the same island is just as dangerous as their staying at the same hotel. They never understood the meaning of amicable divorce.''

"You need to express your innermost feelings, Quinn. I know you'd feel better if you did."

It was times like this she hated dating a clinical psychologist specializing in family matters. He always insisted on analyzing everything to death and there were days when she just wanted to leave it alone.

"Alan, I'll feel much better once I reach the Crystal Falls Lodge. I'll work off my excess energy on the slopes." She carefully smoothed out her bra and folded it before tucking it into a corner of her suitcase.

"I wish you'd stay here for the holidays."

"I need to get away, Alan." She purposely lowered her voice in hopes she would sound more sure of herself since, right now, she wasn't sure of anything. Except the need to drive up north and hole up there until the holidays were over. She wasn't sure why, but this compulsion to go up to Crystal Falls seemed to grow stronger each day.

"If you need to be somewhere for the holidays, come home with me," he urged. "You know how much my parents would love to have you. And with my traveling to all those seminars these past few months, we haven't had very much time together lately."

Not an unreasonable request considering Alan had been trying to persuade Quinn to marry him for the past seven months, fourteen days, fifteen hours and so on. And, for the past seven months, fourteen days, fifteen hours and so on, Quinn had been politely putting him off, even though she continued dating him. She told herself it wasn't fair to keep leading him on. She had to make a decision soon. For a woman who could make split-second decisions in business, she was hopeless when dealing with her own personal problems.

She didn't know why she was acting so indecisive. She did enjoy his company and they had known each other since childhood. In their social circle, Alan was considered a wonderful catch. She reminded herself of his up-and-coming career—there's always someone who needs a psychologist; his excellent family background—his ancestors settled in Boston a hundred and fifty years ago and set up a thriving medical practice; he had no nasty habits and was so faithful he sometimes reminded her of a loyal beagle. The perfect catch. For a woman whose own ancestors arrived on a boat, happy to get work as domestic help, he was manna from heaven. There was only one problem. Every time Alan proposed to Quinn, she promptly headed for a bottle of antacids. If she hadn't insisted he stop proposing every time he saw her, she would have been up to a bottle and a half of tablets a day. Now, she was managing with just half a bottle.

Quinn thought of Alan's mother whose life revolved around the Thursday-afternoon garden club, the opera, the symphony and her volunteer work on various charity committees. Her latest aim in life was to see her son married to Quinn so she could sponsor Quinn to her many clubs. She shuddered in horror at the thought and immediately reached for the tablets on her dresser.

"Alan, reservations at the Crystal Falls Lodge for this time of year are more valuable than gold or diamonds," she reminded him, her teeth crunching down on the tablets as quietly as possible. "You know how hectic work has been lately, and I really need to get away. So I plan to do a lot of skiing, and squeeze in some relaxing."

"And will you be thinking about us?" He lowered his voice to an intimate rumble.

She hoped she wouldn't have to break open a new bottle. She only had a few tablets left in this one.

"Darling, you know how much I love you and want to marry you. Please, Quinn, put me out of my misery and say yes." He went on to tease, "I won't even flinch when you leave your clothes scattered all over the house or don't balance your checkbook for six months."

She looked heavenward for advice. Instead of marrying every man she met the way her mother did, Quinn seemed unable to make a decision one way or the other.

"All right, Alan," she said finally, feeling desperate for a cigarette since the tablets didn't seem to be working. "I promise you I will think very hard about us and I'll give you my answer when I get back."

"Then I'll hope it's the right one," he said, convinced she would have the good sense to say yes. "We're perfect together, Quinn, and everyone knows it. And we both want children."

Yes, she wanted to marry. Yes, she wanted children. But even though Alan was a wonderful man, was he the man she wanted as the father of those children? Everyone thought they were perfect together, but was that reason enough to get married?

"Yes, Alan, you're right."

"Don't worry, darling. I know you'll make the right decision. Call me when you reach the lodge, so I know you've arrived safely. You know I'll worry about you on the road. I wish you'd told me about your plans earlier, so that I could have arranged to go with you."

That was exactly why Quinn hadn't said anything until a couple days ago. She quickly terminated the call and resumed her packing.

She chewed a couple more antacid tablets as the burning in her stomach intensified.

"I have to decide to either marry Alan or put us both out of our misery and just break it off," she said. With a sigh, she dropped down onto the bed and flopped backward against the pillows.

Quinn closed her eyes and visualized the freedom of racing down the slopes with the wind burning into her face. That compulsion to leave her apartment and drive up to Crystal Falls was growing strong again. She jumped up and collected her luggage.

"I need this. I need to know I won't be making a mistake no matter how I decide."

December 9
Ontario Airport, Ontario, California

"I NEED THIS, Dean."

"Bull! What you need is to be with your friends, people who understand you."

Santee looked at Dean Cornell and inwardly laughed at the picture before him. The scruffy ex-L.A. cop had changed from a hotshot detective to a married man. Two years ago, Dean had come down this way to protect Elise Carpenter from her husband's killer, and in the process fell in love with the lady vet and stayed to join in raising her three daughters and their new baby son. How the mighty had fallen.

"You really change your kid's diapers?"

Dean looked affronted at the question. "Of course I change his diapers. I'm damn good at it, too."

"Elise told me the last time you diapered Chad, you used duct tape because the adhesive tabs had you confused."

"It did the job. There was no way that diaper was going to fall off," Dean argued.

"No kidding. She said she had to cut if off him."

Santee thought of the man he called a friend. And the woman who had also become a friend. He envied their happiness.

When he and Elise married, Dean left the Los Angeles police force and now worked with Santee at the sheriff's station. Because of his more than relaxed manner of dress and abundance of charm, he easily gained the confidence of the lower elements. Marriage may have tamed a part of the cocky cop, but he still insisted on keeping his hair shaggy, his clothing disreputable, and doing everything possible to disconcert the normally unflappable Elise. But she couldn't stop loving him any more than she could stop breathing. Furthermore, she gave him the grounding he needed.

"I'm burned-out, Dean," Santee said bluntly. "I'm tired, and there are mornings when I wonder if I should bother even getting up." He recognized the message written on Dean's tense features. "No, I don't have any desire to eat my gun, but I do want to get away for a while. Just rethink my life a bit."

"Fine, rethink it around your friends," Dean argued with concern. "You're not going to find your answers in the toolies of Vermont. Why there?"

He shook his head. "I wish I had an answer for you, but I'm not even sure why. Maybe I just needed someplace new to brush up on my rusty skiing skills. There's nothing earth-shattering going on around here, so I figured it was a good time to use up some of my vacation," he explained.

"What about Debbie?"

Santee looked uncomfortable. "Since I was leaving, I gave her her Christmas gift early. Unfortunately, she wasn't expecting a necklace."

Dean winced. "She was hoping for a ring?"

He nodded. "I'm not ready and she is. So we're not seeing each other anymore."

"I'm sorry, man," Dean commiserated.

"I'm just sorry I hurt her."

Santee turned his head as he heard his flight announced. "Take it easy." He held out his hand.

Dean took it, then stepped forward and gave him a one-armed hug. "*You* take care. There's not many men who're willing to put up with me."

A smile curved Santee's lips. "I'll send you a postcard from Vermont." He picked up his bag and headed for the gate.

"Hey, Santee!" Dean called after him. "What name did you book your flight under?"

He waved his arm over his head. "Detective Santee, what else?"

"Son of a gun!" Dean smiled. "I thought I'd finally learn what his first name is."

Santee boarded the jet and took the window seat assigned to him. As he looked over to the gate, he could see Dean standing there, his hands jammed into the pockets of his beat-up leather jacket. He had a feeling he wouldn't be the same person the next time he saw his friend.

December 10, Midnight
  Vermont

THE SILENCE IN the remote valley was comforting as snow fell to earth to form peaceful drifts untouched by man or beast. Silvery moonlight created shadows across the field. With an abrupt shift in the air, the climate changed to humming expectancy.

The air shimmered in the moonlight with a life of its own. Ethereal shapes twisted and turned in the silvery light until they took on solid form with paved roads snaking through the snow drifts. It wasn't long before the forms looked as if they had always been a part of the countryside.

By morning, the formerly empty valley was covered with small buildings, old-fashioned lampposts dotted the paved roads and the musical ring of voices echoed in the valley. It looked as it had each Christmas for the past few hundred years.

Chapter One

"The National Weather Service is advising everyone near the Crystal Falls area that the snowfall is growing heavier and that anyone who does not have to be out on the roads should remain indoors. This storm has been a surprise for all of us. Even the most experienced drivers could have problems with icy roads."

"Thank you so much for telling me something I already know," Quinn said sarcastically, reaching forward to swipe her sleeve across the fogged windshield. "You'd think for the price they charge for these cars, the defroster would work even if you were in the middle of the arctic circle!" She peered through the clean glass but could only see a blanket of white that obscured any landmarks.

If later asked, she couldn't say if it was intuition or just pure luck that prompted her to slowly brake before she rammed into a dark snow-covered lump. The moment her headlights panned over the large object that she discerned was a car, she saw someone climbing out of the driver's side and waving his arms.

"Jack the Ripper would have more sense than to be out on a night like this." She made sure the passenger door was locked as she rolled down the window an inch. A blast of icy air instantly numbed her face.

"I figured I was going to turn into an icicle before anyone came along," the man gasped. "Any chance of getting a ride to civilization? I can assure you I'm harmless."

She couldn't see much of the face, but the voice seemed innocent enough. And really, she couldn't leave anyone out in this storm. "Get in." She released the passenger-door lock.

"Let me get my bag." He hurried to the car and pulled a bag out of the back seat before returning. "Thanks, I really appreciate this." He fell into the passenger seat and immediately pulled off his gloves, blowing into his cupped hands to warm them. "When they said moderate to heavy snowfall, I didn't expect this."

"I don't think anyone did." Quinn drove slowly around the parked car. "What happened to your car?"

"Don't know. I think something just froze up. It started making weird noises and then finally stopped altogether. I can't imagine why that would happen." His mouth betrayed a ghost of a grin. "This isn't something I come across back home." He turned to look out the window but couldn't see anything but a blanket of white.

"Where's that?"

"Southern California, near San Diego."

Quinn nodded. "You have to worry more about earthquakes than blizzards out there."

"I'd take the earth moving over freezing to death anytime."

She slanted him a wary glance. She wasn't sure if he was deliberately making a provocative comment or an innocent one. It appeared the latter. The dashboard's dim lights didn't show her much of her passenger. Unruly dark hair stuck to his coat collar. His face was about as rawly masculine as you could get, and he possessed a sharp blade of a nose. He was in his early to mid-forties and didn't appear to be the type to spend his days behind a desk. He seemed to be completely comfortable with himself. She'd bet he didn't psychoanalyze every facet of *his* life!

"Have you seen enough yet or do you want to turn on an overhead light for a better look?" His amused question floated across to her.

She flushed. She didn't think he'd noticed her covert glances. "I'm not in the habit of picking up strangers."

"Good. I'm not in the habit of getting stranded in a blizzard, so we're even." He flexed his fingers. "Tell you what, I'll make it easy for you. The name's Santee, I'm a detective with the Riverside County Sheriff's Department, I don't have too many bad habits and have been told I'm relatively harmless."

"I can't imagine who would say that," Quinn said under her breath. The twitch at the corner of his mouth told her he'd overheard her. She tightened her grip on the steering wheel as she felt the car start to slide to the left. Luckily, she brought it back under control.

"You do that very well."

She nodded to his compliment. "Right now, I have no choice. I haven't had a lot of experience driving in heavy storms or on icy roads, but I think I have enough to keep us from skidding into a ditch."

"How about your giving me a few stats?" he asked, lazily unbuttoning his jacket in deference to the heater that had finally roared to life.

Quinn puzzled over the term for a second before recognition hit. "Quinn O'Hara, I'm in advertising and if I was in my right mind, I would be sitting in my warm comfortable apartment in Boston instead of fighting this road." She slowed down even more as the dark shape of a building loomed up ahead. As they coasted past, they could see the gas station was closed up tight. "There's someone smarter than us," she said dryly. "Since there isn't much up here other than the Crystal Falls Lodge, I gather that's where you're going?"

"Yeah, thought I'd get in some skiing."

"Couldn't find any snow closer to home?"

"Wanted a change of scenery." Santee grinned at her quip. "Guess I should have been more careful about what I asked for."

His grin did strange things to Quinn's heartbeat. She didn't want to feel this attraction. Not to a man she'd probably be seeing for the next week or so since they'd be staying at the same small lodge. Still, she couldn't imagine him coming all the way out here alone.

"Are you meeting friends at the lodge?" she asked as casually as she could.

"Nope." He glanced her way. "What about you? Your family spending the holidays up here?"

"My mother is spending them in Jamaica and my father is in Barbados." Her forehead wrinkled. "Or is it the other way around? Either way, I lucked into getting a room at the lodge and, like you, wanted to get some skiing in." She leaned forward and rubbed the frosted window with her sleeve. "When I get back home, I'm taking this car back to that jerk of a mechanic and I'm going to make him eat every nut and bolt," she muttered. "Starting with the heater and the defroster."

Santee chuckled. "That, I'd like to see." This time he took a longer appraisal of his savior. He couldn't tell the color of her hair, only that the short tousled dark-haired mop looked soft and silky. The dim lighting washed out any makeup she might have been wearing and he noticed she had a habit of chewing her lower lip every time the car started to slide across the road. After seeing how well she handled herself, he didn't feel the least bit uneasy about her driving. Hell, she had more experience on these types of roads than he did! The scent of her perfume drifted his way. If he had to be rescued, he couldn't imagine a lovelier rescuer. He straightened up and peered through the windshield.

"It looks like there's a sign up ahead," he announced. "Over there, to the right."

Quinn slowed the car even more, although it was only inching along. "Mistletoe, five miles." She was surprised the sign was so easy to read in the heavy snowfall. "Terrific. Mistletoe must be a tree farm or something."

"Never heard of a tree farm having a rotary club." He pointed out the distinctive insignia beneath the sign.

"The lodge is the only residence up this way." Quinn looked down at the clock blinking in the dashboard and realized it had taken an hour to go a mile and a half. "But right now, I'm about ready to settle for a shack. Maybe they'll have a gas station that can tow your car in. Keep an eye out for a turnoff or something."

Quinn felt her back muscles tighten as they continued down the road.

"At least you don't have to worry about being rearended," Santee commented.

"Yes, I do. With the snow falling so thick, I doubt anyone would be able to see the taillights until it was too late." She rotated her neck to ease the stiffness.

They had no concept of time as Santee watched for further signs and Quinn concentrated on the road ahead, trying not to think about her passenger. She sternly reminded herself she was up here to consider

Alan's proposal, not to drool over a stranger. Still, what could be more romantic? Here they were, alone in the car, snow falling around them, their chance of freezing to death swiftly increasing unless she could find a safe place to stop.

"There's a sign with an arrow pointing to the left," Santee said, breaking into her disturbing thoughts.

"Terrific, a slide to the left." She grimly applied herself to her task. "Just cross your fingers that we don't slide too far and land in a ditch."

"At least we can call for help." He nodded in the direction of her car phone.

"Only if we yell real loud. I tried it a couple hours ago and all I got was static. Probably because of the storm," she explained, surreptitiously flexing her stiff fingers.

Silence hovered in the car as they crept down the road.

"I don't ever recall any mention of a town around here," Quinn commented as she again wiped the windshield. "With our luck, it's probably a tourist attraction that's only open during the summer."

"Positive thinker, aren't you?"

"With the way my life has been going lately, that *is* positive."

Quinn noticed Santee had unbuttoned his jacket and unzipped the inner flap, revealing what appeared to be a rock-hard stomach. Her own stomach took another lurch that rivaled the effects of riding a roller coaster.

What was wrong with her? It wasn't as if she hadn't seen a man's body before. All right, perhaps she hadn't seen a man like this Santee before. But then, she didn't have the opportunity to come in contact with too many cops.

Alan, think Alan, she silently reminded herself. She immediately felt burning acid form in her stomach. She was beginning to believe her stomach upsets were a sign.

Quinn had to keep a light foot on the accelerator as she guided her car up a slight incline. When they reached the top, she had to literally stop herself from stomping on the brake pedal.

"What in the world—?" she murmured, staring at the magical sight below.

"Thought you said there wasn't another town around here," Santee commented, staring at the brilliantly lit village that seemed to beckon to them.

"Not that I knew of, and I've been visiting the lodge for the past eight years." She chewed on her lower lip. "I don't understand it, but I won't turn down a good thing, either." The prospect of a cup of hot coffee and some hot food spurred her into action.

Welcome to Mistletoe.

The headlights tracked the large sign with its bright green ornate-script lettering as they swung past it. Ironically, the heavy falling snow they'd battled the past few hours was absent here. The drifts along the cleared road were gentle ones and sparkling white in the night.

"This doesn't look like something that sprang up overnight," Santee told her as he looked at cottages decorated with lights and wreaths hung on lampposts that looked old-fashioned but burned with modern electricity. People bundled up against the cold strolled down the street calling out greetings to friends and stepping inside open shops.

"There's what looks like a restaurant up ahead. Why don't we stop there and I'll treat you to a cup of coffee," Santee told her.

"Make it an entire pot and you have a deal." She found a parking lot next to the building that stated it was the Mistletoe Inn and Dining Room.

Quinn pulled her wool cap over her head before she climbed out of the car, not caring if it mussed her hair. She groaned as her feet hit the pavement and needles of feeling ran up her legs.

"I feel like a pretzel." Santee stretched his arms over his head. He walked around to the driver's side and took Quinn's arm. "I don't think you want to fall on your face after making it this far," he explained.

"True." As they walked under the oval sign identifying Mr. and Mrs. Hollis Berry as proprietors, Quinn noticed the painted letters were actually twisted sprigs of mistletoe.

"I don't know about you, but I'd say they really believe in celebrating Christmas around here," she commented. She sucked in a breath as warm air hit her face when they walked inside.

"Hello there! My name is Mae Berry." A smiling plump silver-haired woman bustled their way. "Are you here for dinner?"

"Sounds good as long as it's hot," Santee replied, reaching out to assist Quinn as she shrugged off her coat and pulled her cap off her head, stuffing it into her coat pocket. He hung both on one of the available hooks by the door.

"Landsake, of course it's hot," she tittered, leading them into the dining room. "You both look tuckered out."

"We've been battling the beginning of a blizzard," he explained. "It looks like it hasn't hit you so far."

"The valley's protected against most storms." She led them to a corner table. "We're serving pot roast tonight with scalloped potatoes, French-cut green beans. The soup is vegetable, and there's pumpkin pie for dessert."

Santee glanced at Quinn.

"Right now, I'd eat the cow," she confessed.

"Coffee for both of you?" Mae asked. She beamed as they both nodded. "I'll have Edna bring you a carafe first thing."

Quinn looked around with great interest. "I feel as if I've stepped inside the land of Christmas past, present and future." She nodded toward the tree whose top was covered by a delicate golden haired angel. Shiny gold, green and red balls along with twinkling lights were its decorations. Christmas carols played softly in the background. "All we need are a few elves running around."

"Good evening, I'm Edna, your waitress." A cheerful woman with curly dark hair deposited a thermal carafe and two china cups in front of them on the table.

Quinn tried hard not to stare at the woman who was barely five feet tall. With her bright green print dress covered with a white lace apron, she looked like the elf Quinn had just mentioned.

"Would you care for soup, salad or both?"

Both replied they'd like the soup and the bubbly waitress left them.

Santee grinned. He leaned across the table and whispered, "At least she wasn't wearing bright green curly-toed slippers."

"I'm not used to seeing so many cheerful people in one place," she whispered back. "It makes you think they're all on some kind of happy syrup or something."

Santee's chuckle sent warm flutters straight to her stomach. "Think Scrooge would have come to his senses sooner if he'd been sent here instead of meeting those three ghosts?" He picked up the carafe and poured coffee into both cups. He indicated the cream pitcher and sugar bowl. Quinn shook her head to both.

"I doubt it. He needed a good scare." She sipped the steaming brew, sighing contentedly as the welcome warmth spread through her body. "I have to admit this is a lovely room."

At that moment he was too busy admiring something much more interesting than the room. Quinn's sapphire blue sweater brought added color to her cheeks and highlighted her eyes. He liked the fact that she hadn't worried about how she looked the moment she got inside. She merely ran her fingers through her hair without the benefit of a mirror. The cold air had put color in her cheeks and a sparkle in her eyes, which turned out to be a lovely shade of blue tempered with a hint of gray. He noted a black opal ring graced her right hand, a matching pendant swung just above her breasts and opals dotted each ear. She looked up, eyes frozen on his. There was no ignoring the intensity in his gaze.

"Trying to remember what wanted poster you saw me on?" Her voice came out much huskier than she intended.

"Trying to figure out how I got so lucky to be rescued by such a lovely woman."

It wasn't the first time a man had complimented Quinn, but it was the first time she felt such a strong reaction to the words. Or was it a strong reaction to the man?

The lighting showed her a man in his early forties with black hair that only showed a few strands of silver, dark brown eyes and skin bronzed by heritage as much as by the Southern California sun. His gaze was sharp and shrewd, his jaw strong, and every inch of him was so male it shrieked the word. She couldn't help but notice the admiring looks he was receiving from the female diners. Probably because of the cinnamon-brown wool sweater that molded his broad shoulders.

Quinn, who usually didn't lack for words, suddenly found herself tongue-tied. She looked up with a grateful smile when Edna set a bowl of soup before her.

"Now don't worry about hurrying," she told them with a bright smile. "You just relax and enjoy your food."

"I have to admit that getting back on the highway for the lodge is the last thing I want to think about," Quinn said, picking up her spoon.

"I know what you mean. I've never felt a more welcoming atmosphere."

"I don't think everyone agrees with you." She looked at a neighboring table where a stocky, gray-haired man with a scowl marring his features sat with a woman whose dour expression was just as daunting. A girl, who couldn't have been more than six or seven, sat between them and looked as mournful as they looked angry.

"If you'd listened to the travel advisories, this wouldn't have happened," the woman hissed at her husband. "The girl should be home in bed."

"Gramma, I want Mommy." The little girl sighed. She stared down at her plate, her lower lip quivering as if she was about to cry.

"Stop that sniveling! I won't say this to you again, Alice," she told the girl coldly. "Your mother isn't fit to raise you. That's why you'll be living with your grandfather and me instead of with her. Then we'll be sure of your having a proper upbringing."

Alice's eyes flashed as she looked up at her grandmother. "You just don't like Mom 'cause she married Dad."

The woman's features grew so still they looked carved from stone. "We do not have scenes in public, Alice. You'd do well to remember that."

Quinn felt earth-shattering shock overtake her as she studied the little girl. The child's green velvet jumper with red holly berries decorating the straps and the white lace-trimmed blouse could have been a duplicate of the outfit Quinn had worn at that age. Even the little girl's curls restrained by a green velvet hairband seemed so familiar. For one moment she felt as if she were looking at herself at that age. And she had been just as unhappy back then. She felt the urge to run over and gather the little girl up in her arms and assure her everything would be all right.

She kept sneaking glances toward the other table as she found herself unable to stop looking at the unhappy little girl. "Cinderella's stepmother was a sweetheart compared to that crone. She could probably give Scrooge lessons on how to ignore Christmas." She started to pick up her spoon and had to quickly put it down because her hand was shaking so badly.

Santee nodded. "Ironic that someone that sour ended up in a town filled with so much Christmas cheer."

"I doubt she's going to allow any of that holiday cheer into her cold heart," she muttered. "She'd probably just send all that goodwill whimpering in a corner."

As Edna served their main course, Santee and Quinn started to relax enough to exchange more bits and pieces about their lives.

"My parents have gotten married so many times that the holidays are usually their idea of a perfect time for a honeymoon," Quinn explained. "Christmas didn't mean all that much to my family. I usually spent it with whichever parent wasn't newly married at the time or with my grandmother when neither could be bothered with me." She suddenly laughed, even though her words weren't all that humorous. She ducked her head. "I can't believe I said all that."

"For some people, it's easier to reveal things to strangers than friends," he said quietly. "Especially when you don't expect to ever see them again. My grandmother on my dad's side observed Christmas strictly as a holy day and anything else was considered heresy, while my parents wanted us kids to experience all the joys the holiday had to offer. I admit most of us tend to forget just why we celebrate December twenty-fifth, but it's still hard getting kids to understand."

"And here we are in a town simply overflowing with Christmas cheer," she said, smiling. "In fact, it makes you think you've fallen into a holiday movie."

He grinned.

"Mmm, this is wonderful." Quinn used her fork to slice a mouthful of pumpkin pie and swirled it with some of the cinnamon whipped cream before she popped it into her mouth.

"You got a little overzealous with the whipped cream, unless you're saving that little bit on your cheek for later," Santee murmured, reaching across the table and removing the dab by her mouth with his finger and touching it to his tongue.

Quinn was positive her heart stopped when he touched her. And it rapidly returned to life as she watched him taste the cream that had just been on her skin, taste it as if he were tasting her. She suddenly felt light-headed and wished she knew what to blame it on. But she did know. No one but the man seated across from her could have caused this flutter in her heart.

The door blew open and a man who could only be described as a roly-poly dressed in a sheriff's uniform walked in. He stopped to have a few words with Mae Berry before walking into the dining room.

"Excuse me, folks." He nodded toward the people he obviously didn't know. "We just got word a tree fell over onto the road leading back to the highway. I'm afraid it's completely blocked off."

"Are you saying we won't be able to leave here?" the dour-faced woman said sharply.

"Yes, ma'am, that's exactly what I'm saying." He smiled. "But I spoke to Mae and she said there's plenty of room available for you."

"Why can't you just move the tree off the road?"

"It's old and big and is going to need special equipment that we don't have," he explained. "I've contacted a highway maintenance crew, but they're so busy with the blizzard that they won't be able to get to the tree right away. I'm sorry if you're inconvenienced."

Quinn looked at Santee. "I guess we should let the lodge know we won't be arriving tonight, after all."

He looked back at her as the words hung between them. Without thinking, she had made them sound like a couple.

He'd been feeling somewhat dejected thinking that once they reached the lodge, he might not see her again. He knew that someone this lovely would be overwhelmed with attention from the male population. The sensation that he was beginning to feel again was pretty nice. He resisted the urge to grin like a crazy idiot. Wouldn't Dean have a field day knowing Santee had found a woman his first day here.

"Yes, I guess we should."

Chapter Two

"Quinn, I'm sorry, but I don't understand what you mean. How can you be stranded in a small town near the lodge because of a blizzard?" Alan asked. "What blizzard? There is nothing on the news about a blizzard in Vermont. I don't even remember a town near the ski lodge. I don't understand any of this, Quinn. Didn't you check for storm advisories before leaving Boston?"

Quinn took a deep breath. She was already tired and now growing a bit irritated, even though Alan was asking logical questions. "Of course I checked the weather reports before leaving, but nothing was said about an upcoming storm. According to the radio, this came up very suddenly. And I already explained about the turnoff I found to a town called Mistletoe. Believe me, it's aptly named. The way it's all decked out for Christmas, it looks like a holiday tourist attraction even though it isn't." By now, she just wanted to curl up in a tub of hot water and then collapse in bed. "Alan, I called you so you wouldn't worry if you called the lodge and found that I hadn't checked in yet.''

"Sweetheart, I'm not chastising you. I'm glad you called me, because I would have worried if I learned you weren't at the lodge. Did anyone tell you how long you'll be inconvenienced?''

"Probably no longer than tomorrow afternoon. Alan, I have to go—there are people waiting to use the phone,'' she lied. She felt suddenly eager to get off the phone. Alan was just showing his concern for her, but she wished he could tone it down. Then she wouldn't feel so guilty as she realized she could never marry him.

"Wait! What's the number there?'' Alan asked.

She glanced at the phone, but the space that usually displayed a number was blank. "I don't know. It isn't printed on the phone. But I'm at the Mistletoe Inn. I doubt there would be any problem getting it from information. I can't imagine there's all that many Mistletoe Inns in this state. Alan, someone wants to use the phone. I'll talk to you later.'' She quickly hung up and leaned against the wall with her eyes closed.

"Boyfriend?''

She opened her eyes and found Santee watching her with a speculative gaze. "Not exactly.''

"Not exactly your boyfriend?'' he pressed.

"A very good friend,'' she clarified. "He knew I was driving up here and I thought I should call him and let him know about the delay.''

"And now you regret it." Santee made it sound more like a statement than a question.

Quinn opened her mouth, starting to argue with him, but she closed it again without saying a word. She'd already decided she'd said more than enough that evening. What had happened to her usually closemouthed self? She decided it must be something to do with the strange events crashing into her life.

"There you are." Mae beamed as she approached them. "I want you two to know we have a lovely suite available for you. It has a perfect view of the mountains... I know you'll be quite comfortable there."

"Oh, we're not married," Quinn blurted out.

"My dear, I may look like I grew up during the Victorian age, but I understand times have changed over the centuries," she assured the younger woman.

"Oh, no, it's not like that at all. You see, I just picked him up on the highway." She groaned as she realized she was only making matters worse. And Santee, damn him, just stood there and grinned as she dug her hole even deeper. She raked her fingers through her hair as she struggled to offer an explanation that made sense. "You see, he had car trouble on the highway and I stopped to help him since it was snowing so hard. In fact, we were hoping to find a towing service around here."

"I'm afraid no one will be able to look after his car until the tree is cleared from the road," she explained with a sympathetic smile. "Well then, I do have two lovely rooms on the third floor you can have. We only want you to be comfortable during this time of inconvenience.''

"I wasn't traveling on a strict timetable," Santee interjected, presenting the older woman with a smile meant to reassure her. "Besides, I've always felt the unexpected can provide the most interesting surprises.''

Mae couldn't help but smile back. "If you'd like, I can show you to your rooms right now.''

"Quinn, if you give me your keys, I'll get our luggage out of the car," Santee offered, holding out his hand.

Quinn handed them over before following Mae upstairs.

"These rooms catch the morning sun and also have a lovely view of the mountains," the older woman chattered as she led the way. "I'm glad you aren't upset by all this. I'm afraid some of our visitors aren't as amiable. That tree has been upright for a good three hundred years, so I guess it felt it was time to lie down for a rest." She chuckled.

"By upset, you must mean the pickle-faced lady and her husband and child?" Quinn murmured.

Mae chuckled as she walked down the hallway and stopped in front of the last door. "Yes, she is a bit on the sour side, isn't she? To be honest, I don't believe she's had much happiness in her life, poor dear. People like that tend to share their unhappiness with others whether it's wanted or not," she said in a confiding tone as she unlocked the door. She walked in, flicking on the light switch and opening a closet door. "The bath connects with the other room, although I doubt you'll have any problem since your friend will be staying in there." She fluffed pillows and straightened the brightly colored quilted comforter. "I'm afraid the telephone only connects with the lobby. We serve breakfast from seven until ten. If you need anything, please let us know. We want you to enjoy your time here." Her smile continued to warm the room even after she left.

Quinn walked over to the window and parted the curtain just enough to have a partial view of the street below. While most of the shops were closed, outside lights still danced in the night and people still walked along the sidewalks, seemingly oblivious to the bitter cold she remembered feeling when she got out of the car.

"Red and green. Interesting color scheme. It's like being inside a Christmas tree."

She turned to find Santee. He deposited her suitcases on the bed and looked around the room.

"Mrs. Berry put me next door," he told her. "I think she's a matchmaker at heart or she doesn't believe that you were brave enough to just pick me up on the highway."

"I think she just has an overactive imagination," she said, not too bothered by having to share the bathroom with him. The way things were going, she figured she was lucky she didn't have to share a *room* with him. Although, the more she looked at him . . .

Santee watched her closely. "Are you all right?"

She shrugged, hoping he couldn't read her thoughts. "Just tired. Thank you for bringing up my bags."

He nodded. "I'll see you in the morning, then."

"Yes. Maybe they'll have that tree moved early and we can get on up to the lodge." She strove for a bright tone but it faded at the end.

"Good night, Quinn."

She heard the soft snick of the door closing behind him. A moment later, she heard sounds beyond the wall. She assumed it was Santee moving around in his room. Funny how a man she'd only known a few hours could fill her thoughts so easily.

"I wonder what his first name is," she mused as she opened her suitcase and pulled out a pair of soft, yet heavy flannel pajamas and a pair of fuzzy socks. If there was one thing Quinn hated, it was to be cold in bed. No matter how high she adjusted her electric blanket, her feet and legs remained cold if they weren't adequately covered. Therefore, each winter, she searched out and bought the heaviest flannel pajamas she could find and always wore warm socks to bed. This particular pair of pajamas was one of her favorites for traveling. They were extra warm to make up for the lack of her electric blanket. She quickly changed into them, tugging the pullover top down over her hips.

She quickly pulled off the comforter, then found two extra blankets in the closet, draping them over the bed before curling up under the covers, anxiously expecting the sheets to be cold. She was surprised, and very pleased, to find them already warm.

"Maybe I should have gone to a tropical island for the holidays, like my parents did," she mused aloud. "I wouldn't have to worry about snow, then. Instead, I could settle for a horrible sunburn and end up looking like a boiled lobster." She reached out and flicked off the lamp. Within minutes her fatigue caught up with her and she was sound asleep.

WITH THE COVERS bunched at his waist, Santee lay in bed with his arms crossed behind his head. Considering the bitter cold outside, he was surprised to find the room warm and comfortable enough to permit him to sleep au naturel, as he usually did.

"This wasn't the trip I'd envisioned," he murmured to the shadowy ceiling. Then he thought about the woman in the next room. "Still, change is good for the soul."

QUINN WASN'T ONE to wake up easily. Never had been. She always set her radio alarm on the loudest rock-music station possible because she was prone to sleep through conventional alarms. Even then, it still took several cups of coffee to turn her into a coherent being. So, she was surprised when she woke up feeling remarkably alert, especially considering the previous day's events.

She looked down at the red-and-green print comforter that was pulled up to her chin. Now that she'd had time to study the pattern, she realized the print detailed the legend of the twelve days of Christmas.

"I guess it's better to sleep under seven swans a'swimming than a bunch of little snowmen," she mumbled, pushing aside the covers and climbing out of bed. She made sure the bathroom was unoccupied before scooting inside and locking the door leading to the other room.

Quinn braced her hands on the counter and peered at her reflection in the mirror.

"Nothing a hot shower won't cure."

She returned to her room long enough to grab her makeup bag. Not wanting to take too much time in deference to Santee, she quickly showered and shampooed her hair, dried it and applied her makeup before dressing in wool pants and a pullover cowl-necked sweater, both in a warm shade of red. She secured a large bronze pin in the middle of the draping fabric. Feeling ready to face the world, she went downstairs in search of coffee.

"Good morning," Mae chirped, walking out of the dining room. This time, her snowy white apron sported red poinsettias embroidered around the edges. "Your young man has already been down and eaten. He's out taking a stroll around town."

Quinn decided it was more politic to ignore the "young man" reference. "You people really throw yourselves into the holiday spirit around here," she commented as Mae snatched up a coffee carafe and cup before placing her at a small table. "It must take you most of the rest of the year to plan all of this."

Her smile widened. "Yes, we have the spirit, all right, but it isn't something we just do during the holidays. We keep the spirit all year around, because we believe it's very important. Now, we have a choice of entrées for breakfast—ham and cheese omelet, pancakes, waffles, french toast or eggs fixed any style you like. And there's orange, tomato or grapefruit juice."

"For someone who gulps down a cup of coffee on her way to work, it all sounds like heaven," Quinn confessed. "I don't know if I could even make a choice."

"Going without breakfast isn't good." Mae patted Quinn's shoulder. "Why don't we just surprise you." She bustled off to greet more newcomers with a cheerful smile and welcoming hello.

She poured herself a cup of coffee and sipped the bracing brew. "How does she do it?" she asked as Edna came up to her table carrying a trayful of food.

"Mae is always like that," the waitress told her, placing a glass of grapefruit juice down and a plate covered by a golden waffle topped with melting butter. A small pitcher filled with warm syrup followed. "She believes if you're pleasant to a body, they're pleasant to you."

"It takes more than that with some bodies," Quinn murmured, nodding toward the trio just entering the dining room. The sour-faced woman was arguing in a low voice with the man.

"I didn't see anything wrong with our accommodations, Clarissa," he murmured as they walked past Quinn's table.

"Andrew, you wouldn't see anything wrong if it hit you in the face," she replied sharply.

Edna wrinkled her nose. "She doesn't believe in tipping, either," she confided. "Feels tipping might make the servants uppity." Her eyes danced with laughter, showing she wasn't offended by the older woman's imperious manner.

Quinn shook her head. "I'd love to introduce her to some people who could give *her* an inferiority complex."

"And I'd like to see it. Yes, ma'am," Edna intoned as Clarissa looked up, frowned and snapped her fingers.

"I see you decided to join the land of the living." Santee settled in the chair across from Quinn. He reached over and picked up her coffee cup, draining the last before refilling it.

"Wouldn't you prefer to have your very own cup?" she asked with a lift of the eyebrow, plucking the cup out of his fingers and frowning at finding it empty.

"I'm not worried. I don't think you have any germs I need to be concerned about." Then he picked up the glass next to her cup and took a sip of her juice. He glanced at her plate. "Not hungry?"

She quickly grabbed her plate and pulled it closer to her. "Stay away from my waffle. I thought you already ate breakfast."

"I did, about—" he consulted his watch "—an hour and a half ago. But since then, I've been walking around town looking it over." He leaned forward. "There sure are a lot of perky people out there."

Her lips tugged in a reluctant smile. "You don't look as if you're exactly dragging your feet this morning."

"Force of habit. I'm used to going on instant alert." He looked up and smiled when Edna set a cup down in front of him and filled it with coffee. "Thank you, Edna. You just saved my life."

"I suppose you want a second meal?" she teased as she refilled Quinn's cup.

"I think I'll just snack off her plate." He nodded toward Quinn. "More fun that way."

"No, you will not snack off my plate." Quinn looked up at the waitress. "Bring him something fast, please. Because if he touches my waffle, I will shoot him."

"Shooting a cop isn't considered good form. Especially this time of year. Santa might not give you what you want," he said in a jovial tone.

She looked at him with disbelief. "No human being is that alert and perky this early. How much caffeine have you had this morning?"

"To be honest, not enough," he admitted. "And I'm not usually this perky, to use your word. In fact, I'm pretty much a serious guy. It must have something to do with the company I'm keeping." His gaze wandered over the delicate cable stitch decorating her sweater. "Very nice."

She could feel her skin tingling under his regard. She wondered how a man could make her skin tingle just by looking at her. "Please stop it," she whispered.

His eyes slowly rose until they met hers. They were so innocent-looking it stunned her. "Stop what?"

"Looking at me as if I were a gourmet meal."

His eyes darkened. "Sounds good to me."

Quinn's appetite was rapidly leaving her, but she concentrated on finishing her food while fighting with Santee over the last piece of bacon.

"You should have ordered your own," she argued.

"You already said you're full," he returned while his hand hovered over the plate.

She slapped it smartly. "It's the principle of the thing."

"The way you two act, a body'd think you were long-time married." Edna chuckled, appearing long enough to whisk away the plates.

That was enough for Quinn. She shot to her feet and headed out of the dining room. Santee followed at a slower pace.

"I hope you won't grow too bored while you're stranded here," Mae said to Quinn as she stopped at the coatrack. "I'm afraid there aren't a lot of activities for people used to a faster pace. We like a quieter way of life around here."

"What little I've seen has only made me want to see more," she assured the older woman as she slipped her coat on. "Besides, a slower pace is sometimes a nice change." She was abruptly aware of warmth close to her back.

"That's something we Californians have learned," Santee chimed in.

Mae beamed at the tall man. "Mr. Santee, you shouldn't have to be so far away from home during the holidays," she chided with a teasing laugh. "Why haven't you snapped up a lovely girl and had lots of babies so you can spend your holidays assembling bicycles and dollhouses?"

Quinn looked up with an arch of the eyebrow. How nice to see the man could be thrown off-balance! "Yes, why?" she purred.

His smile faltered slightly. "You don't meet too many lovely women in my line of work and there are a lot of women who can't handle being married to a cop."

Mae patted his arm. "I wouldn't worry," she assured him. "I have a pretty good idea your ideal woman is close at hand."

As the two moved toward the front door, the older woman laughed out loud. "Look up."

A funny feeling began in the pit of Quinn's stomach and traveled up right along with her gaze as it fastened on a sprig of green leaves and tiny white flowers tied with a red bow that hung over the door. She tried to smile. She tried hard, but her lips refused to stretch into anything but a semblance of a grimace.

"We only…met yesterday." She stumbled over the words, furious that her usually quick brain couldn't come up with something better.

"It's Christmas," Mae reminded her. "And mistletoe is a tradition that cannot be ignored. Especially here."

Quinn silently appealed to Santee for help. She should have known better.

"Yeah, Quinn, it's Christmas. Let's keep with tradition, shall we?" he murmured, gently taking hold of her arms and pulling her slightly resisting body toward his. He lowered his head and whispered the lightest of kisses across her barely parted lips. She swore she could feel it down to her toes. The sudden flare of fire in his eyes told her she wasn't the only one who experienced that sizzle in the veins.

Santee stood back and gripped her arm. "Come on," he said in a suddenly tight voice.

"You'd probably enjoy touring Rudolph's farm," Mae called after them in her bright voice.

"That woman is too cheerful," Quinn muttered, then realized she was practically being dragged down the street. "Wait a minute!" She dug in her heels until he halted. "Do you see a leash on this neck?" She pointed to that part of her anatomy.

His eyes lingered on her throat in a heated visual caress. "No. Any reason why I should?"

"Then don't try to drag me everywhere as if I was a pet poodle!" She dug her hands into her pockets and pulled out her gloves, quickly smoothing them on and jamming her knit cap over her head. "I can walk very well under my own power, thank you very much. I've been doing it for quite some time now."

He watched her with a smile tugging his lips. "I thought most women stood in front of a mirror to put on those caps, so they could make sure it didn't mess up their hair."

"Trust me, there's no way to muss up this mop. It's so thick I have to wear it short because it takes so long to dry otherwise," she mumbled, brushing a stray lock from her eyes. "And do us both a favor, if it happens again, don't give in to that woman's cute little whims about mistletoe."

"When a woman stands under mistletoe, she has to be kissed. You were standing under it. We weren't supposed to ignore the tradition." He was rapidly learning she was fun to tease and rapidly learning he might not be so burned-out, after all.

"Then I'll make sure not to stand under it again. Let me explain to you that I'm in a long-term relationship and we're practically engaged." She drew what little composure she still retained around her like a tattered cloak.

For a fraction of a second, some undefinable emotion blazed in Santee's eyes. Then he smiled. That very male, very smug smile that unnerved Quinn almost as much as his kiss had.

"Well, sweetheart, I'd suggest you rethink that long-term relationship because the man you're involved with doesn't seem to be doing his job right," he rumbled in her ear. "No man in his right mind would allow such a loose term as 'practically engaged.'"

"Alan is very happy with our relationship the way it is, thank you," she said, stung that he spoke the truth. "As if it's any of your business. Which it isn't." She should have known he wouldn't stop there. He hadn't yet!

"Not the way I see it." He loomed over her. "You don't have the look of a woman who's been well and truly loved, Quinn, and no man worth his salt lets his woman travel the countryside alone. If you were mine, we'd either have made this trip together or forgone it for a place a hell of a lot more comfortable than a car."

Quinn felt hypnotized by both his words and the way his mouth moved as he spoke. Her usual easy way with words deserted her every time Santee said something provocative, and now, her imagination had fired up full force as seductive pictures began flashing before her eyes in quick succession.

There was no snow around them, only snowy white sheets. And it wasn't cold, it was hot. It was two entwined naked bodies on the sheets that caused the heat. Her eyes widened as the mental vision started to turn even more explicit. She quickly closed her eyes in hopes of banishing the image. She should have known better. It only returned in full living color. This never happened any of the times she was with Alan! Her eyes popped back open.

"Too late, I already saw it." His murmur stayed between them. "Makes you wonder if fate somehow brought us here instead of to the lodge where there was a chance we might not have seen each other again."

Quinn snapped her eyes wide open. "I don't believe in fate. I never carried a rabbit's foot for luck, I don't hunt for four-leaf clovers or keep a lucky charm on me or throw salt over my shoulder if I spill it. The way I look at it, you have to make your own luck. It doesn't just come to you."

"I never believed in fate, either, but the more I consider what's happened the last twenty-four hours, the more I think I should revise that opinion."

Chapter Three

Santee took hold of one of Quinn's hands and tucked it into his jacket pocket, wrapping his own around her fingers so she couldn't easily pull it free.

"What do you say we follow Mrs. Berry's suggestion and check out good ole Rudolph's farm? Feed the reindeer and all that."

Quinn blinked. She was discovering it was becoming more difficult to come back to earth after one of Santee's startling statements. Again she wondered what had happened to her usual quick mind that generally came up with quick retorts. That is, it did before she met Santee. Now she could barely walk and chew gum at the same time! Just the man's presence did strange things to her nervous system. It took every ounce of control to keep her mind on track. She wildly searched her brain for something, anything, to talk to him about.

"You never said whether Santee was your first or last name."

"No, I didn't," he replied cheerfully.

She dug in her heels the minute he started to move. "Well?"

"Well, what?"

She took a deep breath. "Is it your first or last name?"

He leaned down and, his warm breath tickling her ear, whispered, "Why don't you guess?"

Quinn couldn't understand what was happening to her. Proximity to Alan had never caused these unsettling feelings she was experiencing. Yet after knowing Santee for barely twelve hours, she was on an emotional roller-coaster ride that she feared would change her life if she allowed it.

"Men who refuse to divulge their full names are usually guilty of something. How do I know you're a real cop?" She looked up at him with narrowed eyes.

"You can call Riverside County Sheriff's Department or call the Lake Elsinore station. There's a Dean Cornell there who will vouch for me."

She rolled her eyes. "He's probably as unorthodox as you seem to be." She held up her free hand. "Wait, don't tell me. He's a rebel, drinks, cusses and carouses with the best of them, looks more like a crook than a cop. Has a new woman every night."

He chuckled at her unconsciously correct perception of his friend. "Insults he can live with. In fact, he'd feel highly complimented by your description. Although his wife might have something to say about the new woman every night. He's also the father of a baby boy and stepfather to three girls, two of them teenagers. Yeah, he's a wild one, all right—usually when one of the girls stays out too late or her date gets a little too friendly.'' He gently tugged on her hand as they continued down the sidewalk, their hips bumping companionably. "I'd rather talk about you. Tell me more about the advertising game."

"And here I thought I was about to hear something wild about you California cops." She heaved a dramatic sigh. "All right, what can I tell you about the advertising business? It's very fast-paced, hectic, an insane way to make a living. But it's also very satisfying when you see your ideas in print or on film." She unconsciously flexed her fingers before lacing them through his again, enjoying the warmth of his palm surrounding her hand. She paused to look inside a shop window. "Look at her. Isn't she beautiful?" she breathed, pressing her free palm against the glass.

Santee looked past Quinn's shoulder at the clear acrylic shelves displaying baby-faced cherubs topped with red-flowered crowns, mischievous-looking elves carrying tiny toys and delicate-featured angels with silver or gold airy wings fanned out behind them. But he couldn't miss what caught Quinn's eye. In the center of the display was a golden-haired angel wearing a pearl silk gown edged with narrow glittering gold braid. Her slender arms were raised as she held a small red candle between porcelain palms. But it was the ethereal expression on Quinn's face as she stared at the angel that captivated Santee.

"They won't be open until this afternoon." He pointed to the small printed sign on the door. "Want to take a closer look then?"

"I don't think so." She turned and started down the sidewalk, pulling him along behind her.

"I bet it would make a nice addition to the decorations you already have," he persisted. "One of my deputies buys several new collectible ornaments for her tree every year. Says in a few years she'll have to have a second tree to hold all of them. Another woman at work looks for anything that has mice in it. I'm surprised her cat hasn't gone nuts with all the mice she's collected by now," he said dryly.

Quinn shrugged. "I don't decorate my apartment for the holidays."

Santee pulled her to a stop. "You don't put *anything* up?"

She couldn't understand his surprise. "I didn't realize it was a crime not to decorate for Christmas."

"It's not. It's just that everyone I've ever known has put up some kind of decoration for the holidays."

"Well, I happen to not be one of those," she said firmly. "And you don't have to look at me that way either! It's not as if I'm some kind of Scrooge, or something. I don't put them up because then I don't have to worry about taking them all down later. Furthermore, I'm rarely home and I seem to go to more parties than I give during this time of year. I do my share of entertaining during the summer and let others have their parties now."

He shook his head in disbelief. "You don't even put up a tree? A wreath on the door? Nothing?" He still couldn't take it in.

"Not a thing, and stop acting as if it's the crime of the century!" she retorted, shifting uncomfortably under his stunned regard. "Not everyone goes all out for Christmas. Just because retail goes nuts this time of the year doesn't mean everyone has to."

Santee thought of the Christmases he'd shared with friends and family over the years. Especially when Dean pulled him into the family circle with the claim that he needed as much testosterone backup as possible. If there was one thing Elise enjoyed celebrating, it was Christmas. She poured all her energy into making the holiday more memorable than the year before.

"Okay, okay." He held up his hands in the classic pose of surrender. "Not another word."

Quinn eyed him suspiciously. "You didn't strike me as the kind of guy who backs down so easily."

"There are some things I won't back down on. Do you mind if we keep moving?" He leaned over to whisper in her ear. "I'm freezing my butt off out here!"

She shook her head with mock pity in her eyes. "You Californians need to build up your blood when you're building up your muscles. This is considered a warm day compared to what we usually have up this way."

"This from the woman who's wearing thermal underwear."

Quinn bit her lip before she could ask how he knew that. She didn't think she wanted to know the answer. "Well then, let's get going before you freeze the rest of your body parts off." She withdrew her hand from his pocket and set off at a clip that would make a drill sergeant ecstatic.

Santee happily ambled on behind her, content to just enjoy the view of her slim figure walking at an energetic pace. Even her bulky clothing didn't hide her natural grace. "Do you want to stop for some coffee?" he called after her.

Quinn turned around in time to see Santee gesture toward a bakery on the other side of the street. She wasn't about to admit she was cold, too. Even with the thermal layer under her sweater and wool pants, she could feel the cold numbing parts of her body. She didn't hesitate with her answer.

"Definitely."

They stepped into the bakery and inhaled the warm and yeasty aroma of fresh-baked bread along with the sweetness of warm pastries and cookies.

Quinn pulled her cap off and opened her coat as she headed for the glass case.

"Two large coffees, please," Santee told the smiling woman standing behind the case. "And I wouldn't be surprised if the lady could be persuaded to have something else."

"Raspberry danish," Quinn immediately decided, hoping he hadn't noticed she was practically salivating on the unsmudged glass. She mentally reminded herself that the cold burned more calories than heat. "Two."

Santee carried the cups over to a window table while Quinn accepted her snack from the clerk.

"Are you sure you don't want anything?" she asked as she slid onto the chair opposite him.

He shook his head. "Not me. I prefer caffeine jitters to a sugar high any day."

"And here I thought you cops spent half your lives at the doughnut shop."

Quinn bit into the flaky pastry. She closed her eyes, moaning happily as the sugar and tart raspberry filling exploded in her mouth. Sensing she was being watched, she opened her eyes. Santee was looking at her with an expression that had nothing to do with friendly observation. She blamed the shop's warm interior for the heat suddenly flowing through her body.

"Are you sure you don't want some?"

He picked up a napkin and leaned across the table, carefully dabbing sugar and raspberry filling from the corners of her mouth. "I don't think you'd appreciate the way I'd take my share."

Now she knew the heat wasn't just coming from the warmth of the shop. Erotic pictures of how he would share her danish started flashing through her head. What was it about this man?

"We hardly know each other," she finally said feebly.

"People on a first date know less about each other than we've already learned."

She felt breathless. "We aren't on a date."

"Okay, a getaway." His eyes fastened on her mouth.

Quinn looked around, helpless to find a reason for the constriction in her lungs. This is all so crazy, she mused, tearing a piece of the danish apart with her fingers. This whole odd sensation must have something to do with the town and our strange circumstances. None of this has been normal. She quickly turned toward the clerk who was pretending not to be watching the tense exchange between the couple. "Excuse me, but have you heard if that tree that fell across the road has been moved yet?" There, she sounded bright and chirpy as if nothing had happened.

The woman's cheerful smile resembled Mae's and Edna's. "All we've heard is that the crews haven't been able to get to it yet because of the storm. I can imagine you're grateful you aren't stranded in your car."

Quinn didn't quite agree with the woman's statement about being grateful. Not with this powerful attraction to Santee she was feeling. "Would you have any idea when they'll get out there?"

"No, I'm sorry."

Quinn finished her two pastries, but she didn't enjoy them as much as she had when she'd taken that first bite. She finally decided it was time for her to get back into her aggressive mode. After all, she thought, I'm an expert in the advertising game. I'm used to thinking on my feet, making snap decisions. That should keep my emotions safe for a while. Santee's eyes on her interrupted her thoughts.

"Tell me, Santee, are you always this direct?"

"It's how I get my answers." He tipped the cup back, finishing the last of his drink.

"I bet you run a police check on the women you date."

"Only to see if they've ever been brought in for murdering past dates." He grinned. "That would make me a little nervous. What if she didn't like the place I took her to for dinner? I might end up getting more than I bargained for when I take her home."

Quinn had to laugh at the idea of a woman angry enough to attack Santee for taking her to the wrong restaurant. "It would put a new light on the idea of dates from hell," she said. "I work with a woman who's convinced there isn't a decent man out there. Her last date asked her to attend a party with him. He just neglected to mention that it was a birthday party for a friend's cat."

Santee chuckled. "Was the cake made out of liver?"

She shook her head, grimacing. "Just as bad. Salmon with tuna frosting."

"Maybe that's why I hate dating," he admitted. "I'm more into long-term relationships. I quit racking up notches on the bedpost when I was barely out of college. Being a party animal was never my style."

"I'm not that fond of it, either," she said in a low voice, methodically folding her napkin into intricate pleats. At that precise moment, she could feel that old burning in the pit of her stomach as she thought of Alan. Dear sweet Alan who loved her more than she could ever love him.

Santee watched her closely. "I'm surprised some guy hasn't snapped you up."

"Maybe I don't want to be snapped up!" The moment she responded, she realized her mistake.

"You know, if you relaxed a little bit more around men, you might find out that we're not so bad, after all."

She grabbed her small leather bag and stood up. "I'm not a suspect to interrogate, Detective," she muttered, rapidly moving toward the door.

Santee muttered a curse under his breath as he stood up and hurried after her.

"Do us both a favor and find your own ride up to the lodge when the road is clear," she informed him when he caught up.

"Guilt makes a person nervous," he commented, refusing to rise to her bait.

"I am not guilty about anything, nor am I nervous!" she snapped, refusing to look his way. She'd never run the gamut of so many emotions in so little time, and she didn't think she liked it happening. She pulled out her knit cap.

"If you're not nervous, why are you pulling your cap into the next larger size?" he asked with bland innocence. He noticed the morning wind had ruffled her hair into loose curls. He had to stuff his hands into his pockets so he wouldn't be tempted to touch her. He doubted she would appreciate it right now. "Fine. So tell me about your boyfriend."

"What boyfriend?"

By now, Santee knew he wasn't going to mince words with Quinn. Not when he'd already decided he wasn't going to allow her to get away from him that easily. "The one you've got and won't talk about. I like to know what I'm fighting."

Quinn wasn't about to go into that. She ducked into the first door she came to. Her eyes widened as she took in her surroundings.

Stuffed animals looked down from several rows of shelves while a group of children were clustered around a table set in the middle of the store where they could happily play with a variety of battery-operated toys that barked, clucked, baa'd and growled.

Quinn moved farther into the store and slowly turned in a circle. She couldn't seem to find an end to the place!

"Interesting choice. I would have figured you'd head for the first dress or lingerie shop in hopes I'd be too embarrassed to follow you." Santee's rumble sounded from behind.

"I doubt there's anything on earth that can embarrass you." She headed for the aisle marked Games. She stopped and looked at the long row before her. "This doesn't make sense." She looked at the large assortment of games for all ages. "How could a town this small support a store this large? With this kind of inventory? This is bigger than some of the chain toy stores I've seen."

"They're a tourist attraction. With them touting the Christmas theme, it's logical they'd have a big toy store where a kid could find anything he might want," Santee commented, pulling a child's board game off a shelf and studying the top. He turned the box over in his hands. "Hey! I haven't seen one of these since I was a kid. I didn't know it was still manufactured."

"They probably keep anything that's ever come out so they can fill the shelves. Or, for all we know, these boxes might be shams." She still felt confused as she looked around and walked to the end of the aisle.

Santee pulled down another box and surveyed the contents. "Nope, this game is in mint condition. I bet a collector would pay a small fortune for this. Besides, what's so wrong with having a toy store that carries everything?" He couldn't miss the shock on Quinn's face as she stopped short. She walked in a daze toward several glass shelves holding dolls.

"It can't be," she whispered, putting her hand out, then snatching it back as she stared at one particular doll displayed on a shelf just above her head.

He stopped behind her. "Can't be what? Honey, is it the doll?"

Quinn couldn't stop looking up at the ballerina doll dressed in a pastel pink, blue and lavender tutu with spangles of silver scattered across the tulle skirt. Her delicate toe shoes were made of pink silk that echoed the color in the ribbon threaded through her blond chignon. Rose pink lips were pursed and blue eyes seemed to dance with smiling lights at the observer. The first hesitant notes of a familiar tune echoed in Quinn's head.

"I see you've found our sugarplum fairy," a hearty voice boomed from behind. "Lovely, isn't she?"

"But it can't be her," Quinn protested, turning around. Whatever else she was going to say flew out of her head as she stared at the man who'd approached them. She realized she'd been gauche and blushed with embarrassment.

The man they faced was rotund, with twinkling blue eyes, rosy round cheeks and a snowy white beard.

"I'll be damned," Santee breathed, studying the older man. "It's Santa Claus."

"Ah, ah, ah." The man held up an admonishing finger. "Children and their acute hearing, you know. I'd feel very bad if too many came up with last-minute requests I couldn't fill."

"She can't be here," she cried.

"Santa" smiled. "Why not?"

"Because she was my doll when I was eight," Quinn blurted out, pointing at the shelf just above her head. "My mother took me to the ballet to see the *Nutcracker Suite* that Christmas. She gave me the doll that year because I loved the ballet so much and the doll's costume was similar to the dancers'." She pressed her fingertips against her forehead as too many conflicting emotions rushed through her brain.

"I would think there was more than one doll manufactured back then," Santee cut in, startled by the vehemence in her voice and manner. Not to mention worried when her eyes looked slightly wild. It didn't take a mind reader to see she was more than a little upset over seeing something from her past. He'd hazard a guess there was more to her story.

Her eyelids flickered as doubt crept in. "Yes, of course," she murmured. A faint shade of red crept up her throat. "I don't know what I was thinking."

"It's natural you would feel shock at seeing an old friend," the older man assured her, patting her shoulder. "Now, is there any other way I may help you? My name is Kris and I own The Toy Factory."

"Appropriate name," Santee murmured. When Quinn looked at him questioningly, he clarified, "His name and the shop's name. Although, in this town, I shouldn't be surprised by anything with a Christmas theme that comes up."

"We believe in keeping the spirit of Christmas all year around," Kris explained, smiling at the couple.

"Love to your fellow man?" Santee quipped.

Kris took him seriously. "Exactly!"

Santee looked down at Quinn who was still studying the ballerina doll with a fervid gaze. "I can understand why."

"It's so strange seeing her here," she murmured, deaf to their conversation as she lost herself in memories. "She somehow got lost when my mother and I moved away after my parents got their divorce. I cried for almost a week because I was convinced it was my fault she was gone."

Just as the little girl she'd been probably felt it was her fault her parents had split up, Santee thought.

Kris reached up with remarkable ease and brought the doll down, carefully unclasping the special stand she was attached to. "Then I think you need this old friend more than we do."

Quinn shook her head slightly as if unsure she'd heard correctly. "I don't understand."

"She's yours, Quinn," he said gently, holding the doll out. "I don't think any other girl could cherish her the way you could."

Quinn put her hands behind her back. She was still so dazed she didn't stop to wonder how he knew her name. "I can't take her," she said in a barely audible voice. "It's not right."

Kris studied her with gentle curiosity. "Why not?"

Quinn spoke as if she were separate from her thoughts. As if another person had taken over her will. "Because there's always a little girl out there who needs a friend." She turned away abruptly and walked out of the store.

Santee spun around as if to catch her arm, then stopped as if someone had held him back.

"Little girls usually consider their dolls their best friends," Kris said in a quiet voice instead of his usual warm rumble. "Boys have trouble understanding that, even though they need a security companion, too. Yours was your pitcher's mitt, wasn't it?''

Santee looked back at the older man. "That's a pretty good guess for a guy who probably plucked that idea out of the air. Are you sure you're only a toy-shop owner?"

Kris lifted his shoulders as if to say, "Am I?" He looked so innocent Santee couldn't help wondering what he was thinking.

Santee left the store with a cautious eye over his shoulder every step of the way. Once outside, he looked both ways but couldn't catch a glimpse of Quinn.

"Damn," he muttered, flipping a coin and heading down the street. "Women who practically talk like a Christmas carol, men who look like Santa Claus and own a toy shop, an entire town that looks like something out of a storybook. I should have driven up to Mammoth to ski instead of flying back here just because I felt I needed to get out of the area."

But if you had gone to Mammoth, you wouldn't have met Quinn. Admit it, you haven't met any other woman who fascinates you as much as she does. Debbie included.

He stopped to peer inside a shop named Noelle's Gifts and heaved a sigh of relief when he discovered the object of his search.

"My life was much easier when my brain didn't spout logic."

Chapter Four

Quinn took elaborate care in studying the label attached to the hand-crafted pillow that gave the name of the craftsperson, although, if asked, she wouldn't remember one word she'd read. She traced the red silk poinsettia stitched on the front with her fingernail but didn't feel it as her senses warned her that Santee had stepped into the shop and was headed straight for her.

"Are you sure you want something that looks like a Christmas decoration in an apartment you don't decorate for the holidays," he commented offhandedly, looking over her shoulder at the pillow.

"Red figures very prominently in my color scheme." She kept her voice stiff and standoffish in hopes he'd take the hint. She should have known better. She was still reeling from having stumbled into a once-important part of her past. She wished she could understand how a doll she hadn't seen in twenty years could affect her so strongly. And now with Santee standing so close to her, she felt light-headed. Were her hormones so out of whack that she couldn't stand next to a man without feeling as if she were going to jump his bones.

His dark eyes swept over her. She knew he saw the way her fingers crushed the edges of the pillow and with the flushed rose of her skin he could probably read exactly what she was thinking.

"Do us both a favor and don't act like a cop looking for something that isn't there," Quinn tautly suggested as she carefully set the pillow back on the display. She needed to get away from him. She moved on to inspect tablecloths that ranged from snowy white linen to bright red or green. "I don't know how a person could stand seeing Christmas things around them all year. You'd think they'd want a change of pace by the time Easter comes around. You know, a few bunnies instead of reindeer, or chicks instead of elves."

"What's wrong with reindeer and elves?"

They both turned to see a young woman dressed in a red print dress. Her tiny white badge clipped to her dress stated her name was Noelle. Quinn noticed her smile was as bright and cheerful as everyone else's in Mistletoe, and her question nothing more than polite curiosity.

"Christmas is only one day a year," Quinn replied. "Doesn't being around the trees and ornaments, hearing the carols all the time and everything else connected with the holiday make it not as special when it does come around?"

"When you were a little girl, didn't you wish Christmas was all year round?"

Santee grinned. "Doesn't every kid want that?"

"And every December, don't you hear and read that people should observe the meaning of Christmas all year round?" Noelle swept her hand around the shop. "That's exactly what we do here. We live the meaning of Christmas. We believe in it."

"Bet that cuts down your crime rate," he quipped.

"We really don't have any crime."

"But you have a police force," Santee pressed, his mind trying to figure that one out. A town with no crime rate? Talk about the impossible! How come news of this crime-free town hadn't reached the law enforcement community by now?

"Rudy is our town sheriff. He basically makes sure we've locked the shop doors at night and that the children aren't out too late at night or haven't wandered away where they might get hurt," Noelle explained. "To be honest, our visitors tend to rely on him more than we do."

"You have that many tourists come through here?" Quinn was incredulous. "No offense, but you're so far off the beaten track, I don't understand how people even know you're here. I know I've never seen any magazine articles or advertisements about Mistletoe. I'd have remembered."

Noelle's sunny smile didn't change. "We don't need to advertise. People find us when they need us." She looked past Quinn's shoulder as someone walked in the door. "Excuse me."

"People find us when they need us?" Quinn muttered in disbelief. "Is she trying to sound like some kind of ancient oracle? Or is she making this place sound so mysterious, yet exciting, we'll tell our friends about it?"

Toward the front of the shop, Clarissa looked down her nose at the younger woman. "My dear girl, I am very experienced in recognizing fine linen, and this tablecloth is not fashioned of the high-quality fabric you claim it is."

"I'm sorry if you don't approve of our stock," Noelle soothed, carefully folding a tablecloth and replacing it on the shelf. "We do try to carry only the best quality."

"I don't approve of shopkeepers pushing off inferior merchandise. They tack a holiday on to it to make it seem unique and then assume customers will buy it." Clarissa flicked her fingers over a round, red, foil-covered container filled with napkin rings fashioned to look like tiny filled toy boxes and another box filled with gaily painted reindeer.

"Gramma, look!" Alice held up a smiling elf figurine. "He looks like my teacher."

Clarissa rolled her eyes. "Put it down before you break it, Alice."

"The old witch," Quinn muttered, seeing the little girl's crestfallen features as she slowly set the elf back on the counter. "She belongs in Salem instead of up here in the land of reindeer and holly."

Catching the tail end of Quinn's words, Clarissa looked her way. "I don't believe you were a part of this conversation."

Quinn ignored the chilling censure in the woman's words. "Considering the way you're acting, I wouldn't want to be," she retorted, advancing on her with fire in her eyes.

"Quinn, I don't think this is a good idea," Santee murmured at the same time as Clarissa's husband was whispering similar words to his wife. Both women ignored both men. The gauntlet had been thrown and was now being picked up.

"You are by far the rudest, most inconsiderate woman I have ever had the displeasure to see," Quinn was the first to verbally attack. "Just because something happens that's beyond your control, you have to disparage everything, and you don't care whose feelings you hurt, do you? Even if it happens to be your granddaughter's."

Clarissa drew herself up to her full bony height and looked down her nose at the younger woman. "You are certainly the last person to speak of rude and inconsiderate!"

"These people are knocking themselves out to make sure we enjoy ourselves here because we're stuck until the road crew can clear that tree away. You act as if they did all this deliberately in some elaborate plan to keep us here as their prisoners." Quinn leaned forward, her hands on her waist. Her body was stiff with a tension that loudly telegraphed she was more than willing to come out punching at any second. "You seem to be a woman who loves to point out others' shortcomings. Perhaps you should think about taking your own advice. You might learn something in the process."

Clarissa's gaze was sharp enough to cheerfully slice Quinn's heart from her body.

"You are a very impertinent young woman who obviously wasn't raised to respect her elders." Her glance swung just behind Quinn's shoulder to take in Santee, easily dissecting his silver-gray ski parka topping worn jeans, and dismissing him as no one of any value.

"People should *earn* respect, not expect it," she snapped. "Maybe I learned something better. Maybe I learned about compassion, instead. And be careful about casting that first stone. It just might fly back and hit you in the face." Quinn noticed the little girl standing nearby watching the heated exchange. Her tiny face was scrunched up in a distress she couldn't have hidden if she tried. She lowered her voice. "You have what appears to be a very sweet little granddaughter. This is the time of year for children. Why not show her what Christmas really is? Show her some fun and laughter, not nitpicking. Don't take away her Christmas so that she hates it and you from now on." She suddenly halted, looking as if she'd been struck.

"My granddaughter is none of your business, and one thing she will learn is that Christmas is nothing more than crass commercialism pushed upon us by retailers." She spun on her heel and stalked off, barely pausing as she grasped Alice's arm to propel her out of the store.

Santee noticed Quinn's stricken expression as she watched the older woman walk away.

"Terrific, Quinn, why not just let it all out," Quinn muttered in self-disgust, finally returning to her old self. "Don't hold anything back."

"Miss." Andrew, Clarissa's husband, touched her arm. "Few people have stood up to my wife the way you did."

She grimaced. "I apologize for being so rude."

He smiled his reassurance. "No, what you said made sense. And hopefully, if she stops to think about the words, she'll realize that." He patted her arm once more before hurrying off.

"Do you think she would have looked at me as if I were a member of the lowest life form if I'd shown her my badge?" Santee asked. "Honey, that lady is one cold fish. She brought back some pretty nasty memories of my fourth-grade teacher, who used to predict that I'd end up in the state penitentiary—and told my parents to prepare for it happening."

She tipped her head back. "I hope she knows you didn't fulfill her dire prediction."

"You bet she knows. I was part of Career Day at the school a couple of years ago and I made a point of going up to see her." He chuckled. "Funny thing is, I think she sees cops in the same light as the crooks." He guided her toward the door and outside. "Come on. Let's get out of here."

"I normally don't do things like that," she apologized as they walked down the sidewalk. "I make a point of being diplomatic. I don't get taken advantage of easily, but I also don't usually lash out. I just acted on instinct with her. I suppose Alan would approve of my getting in touch with my emotions." She jammed her cap on top of her head and drew on her wool gloves.

"Alan?"

Either she didn't notice the dangerous note in his voice or she chose to ignore it, so she could put some distance between them.

"Yes, we've been seeing each other for quite some time now," she said airily.

"Oh. Is this your almost-fiancé?"

"Maybe."

Santee's expression turned grim as they walked along. Then it cleared as he decided that she was with him, and right now, that's what mattered most. Because he had a feeling that there must be a reason he and Quinn were here. And he was willing to go along with anything fate had planned.

All morning, Quinn had detected a hint of spice in the air and assumed it was coming from the shops until she finally realized it was coming from Santee. She took in a deep breath and realized her mistake immediately. Spice mixed with his own personal scent was incredibly arousing. She was beginning to think the more she was around him, the more she was affected. She looked around for anything to divert her attention from him.

"Look at the street sign!" she said, laughing and pointing at the sign ahead of them.

Santee followed the direction of her finger to see a carved reindeer whose head was topped with a tiny mound of snow announcing they were crossing Prancer Way.

"Now I really feel as if I've just been dropped into the middle of a holiday movie," she said. "I expect Bing Crosby to pop up and start singing 'White Christmas.'"

"Be careful what you say—anything could happen." He glanced down the next road. "Come on, let's see what we can find down this way." He'd grabbed her hand and was pulling her down Elf Lane when he spied a movie theater marquee in the distance.

"*Miracle on Thirty-fourth Street* and *Holiday Inn*," Quinn stated as, hand in hand, they stood on the sidewalk and looked up at the red-lettered marquee.

"Think they'll show *It's a Wonderful Life* and *White Christmas* next week?" he asked.

She giggled. "Probably, and maybe even a Saturday kiddie matinee of *A Charlie Brown Christmas*. Don't you feel this is too much?" She swept her arm out.

He thought about it for a moment. "My baby sister would say it gives her the warm fuzzies. That's her favorite term right now."

"Baby sister? How many do you have?"

He kept his arm around her shoulders as they continued walking. "Four sisters and four brothers. I was unlucky enough to be born smack-dab in the middle."

Quinn skidded to a stop, almost throwing Santee off-balance. *"Nine?"* she squeaked, wide-eyed with shock. "Your mother had nine children?"

His smile was touched with a hint of sorrow. "Actually, there were eleven of us, but one was stillborn and I had a younger brother die of complications from measles when he was six. At the time, it swept through the family, putting seven of us in bed, but it hit him the hardest."

"I'm sorry." The look on her face told him this wasn't an empty phrase to her. "Nine children," she mused as they walked. "How many bathrooms did your house have?"

Santee's shoulders shook as his laughter overtook him. He finally had to stop and lean against a building before he lost his balance.

"Only a woman would worry about the number of bathrooms," he choked.

"You may think it's funny, but I bet your sisters didn't," she retorted. "So how many were there?"

He curved his hand around hers and smiled. "One."

"One?" Quinn wheezed, aghast at the conclusion she was drawing. "One bathroom? I'd hate to be in your house in the mornings while you were all getting ready for school. There must have been a lot of battles."

"There was enough of an age difference between all of us kids that not all of us lived at home at the same time," he explained, still leaning against the wall. "And my dad is a real organizer, courtesy of his years spent in the marines. He set up a rotating schedule that we had to stick by or risk being the last one using the bathroom for a month."

She shook her head, still trying to assimilate the shock of learning he had such a large family. She absently kicked at a small mound of snow on the curb left behind after the streets had been cleared of the previous night's snowfall. She was surprised to find it still a pristine white even though there was foot traffic on the sidewalks. "I can't even imagine such a situation. It sounds like something on a TV sitcom."

"Don't you have any brothers or sisters?"

"I have two stepsisters and three stepbrothers." She frowned. "Or is it the other way around? I never can keep it straight. I never really saw much of them. None of my parents' marriages lasted long enough for me to get to know any of them, other than our meeting one another at the weddings." She straightened up and forced a smile to her lips. "If you have such a large family, why are you back here instead of home spending the holidays with them? You've already told me they don't ignore Christmas the way my parents always have." Faint bitterness scored her words.

"I figured it was time for a change. I tend to divide Christmas between family and friends, anyway. Besides, I promised to be back in time for New Year's."

"Unless that maintenance crew forgets to clear the road," she said wryly. "As for New Year's, the people around here don't look like the type to suddenly turn into party animals."

Santee's fingers rested lightly against Quinn's waist as he finally gave in to the impulse that had plagued him all morning. With a faint smile curving his lips upward, he slowly urged her toward him.

"This isn't a good idea," she breathed, glancing right and left as she easily guessed his intent. Part of her wanted him to do it, another part wondered if it was a good idea. The first part was rapidly winning.

"There's no one around," he assured her as their bodies lightly touched.

"You forget that line from the song, 'He knows when you've been bad or good...'" She was aware of the tiny catch in her throat as she felt her curves mold against him as if they recognized him as a long-time lover. Her mind was stunned by the idea.

"I've been good, very good," he murmured, warming her lips with his breath. "What about you?"

"I'm always—" Her words were abruptly cut off by the increasing pressure of his mouth on hers.

Quinn should have been prepared for her body's reaction after what had happened when they'd shared the light kiss under the mistletoe this morning. Except the two kisses were as different as a Fourth of

July sparkler and a nuclear bomb. Heat waves swept upward from her toes, taking over every nerve in her body until she was nothing more than a being filled with sensual awareness. She dug her fingers into his arms in order to keep herself upright because she was positive her knees had turned to jelly.

"Santee!" she gasped when her mouth was freed for scant seconds. She tightened her hold on him, not caring if he had bruises there by that evening. "This is crazy! We're on a public street! People could see us!"

"I told you, no one's around. Besides, I'm showing goodwill toward my fellow man. Better yet, woman." His grin flashed wicked ideas into her brain. "Besides, I've wanted to really kiss you again ever since we met under the mistletoe." His mouth trailed a heated path down the curve of her cheek.

"But I'm involved—" She knew her protest was weak, but she felt she had to make one. To say something. She quickly ignored the acid burning in her stomach.

"No protests, sweetheart." His gaze roamed over her body with lazy grace, effortlessly stripping her clothing away. "In fact, you kiss like a woman who's ready for more." He dipped his head.

"No, I am not!" Quinn pressed her palms against his chest and angled her head away from his. "Santee, this is New England. Land of Puritans and ultra-conservatives—not California, where people believe in letting it all hang out. Around here, people have been hanged for less. Besides, I need to stop before my brain starts feeling like cooked oatmeal."

"Feeling a bit hot and bothered? That's okay, me, too." He bumped his hip against hers. She moaned when she felt his arousal nudging her feminine cradle. The lower part of her body grew heavy with yearning as she unconsciously arched toward him. Turning her face away to take a sane breath didn't help—he just concentrated on her ear, instead. She felt her nerve endings quiver when he began nibbling her lobe.

"The temperature is in the low twenties and that's not even taking in the wind-chill factor," she gasped. "There's no way I could feel hot and bothered in this kind of weather."

His fingers dug into her waist so she couldn't escape him. "What are you so afraid of, Quinn? Are you afraid you'll find out you can't hide behind a bogus engagement?"

"It isn't bogus!" she gasped, pushing herself out of his arms and making sure to stand out of his reach. "Alan proposed to me again right before I left and I promised him an answer when I returned. So there!" She moved forward as if she were going to kick him in the leg, then spun around and marched off with her head held high.

"I should throttle her," he muttered, staring at her retreating back.

"That's one fine woman you have."

Santee turned his head to find Kris standing across the small alley between the two buildings.

"Is she right? Is kissing a woman in public around here a hanging offense?"

"If so, there'd be a lot of good men dead and buried." Kris chuckled. "Take it from a man who's been around a long time. Give her some time to cool off and think things over. She just might come to the conclusion that the man in her arms is a better bet than the one who isn't around."

Santee regarded the white-haired man with a faint niggling of suspicion.

"Exactly who are you?"

Kris smiled. "Just a man who's had plenty of time to study the human race and learn a few secrets."

"And what did you learn?"

"That no matter how long a man lives, he'll never find out just what a woman is thinking. They always find a way to confuse us poor men." His bright blue eyes twinkled merrily. "But then, we men don't make it easy when we have such trouble with our names."

Santee froze. "Wait a minute."

Kris shook his head. "Think about it, son. You know what I mean."

Santee looked away for a second, formulating an argument, but when he turned around to face the older man, he found the space where Kris had stood now empty.

"Where did he go?" he murmured. He looked around but found no door through which Kris could have disappeared. The other man's comment came back to him, along with an earlier comment. How had he known Quinn's name back in the toy shop and sensed how deeply she felt about that doll? And how had he known about his...? "There is no way he could know any of it." He froze as a very strange thought hit him like a freight train. "Is there?"

Chapter Five

"Now, dear, you just sit there and relax with a nice cup of tea," Mae crooned, ushering Quinn into a side parlor and practically pushing her into a chair. "After being out in that horrible cold air all morning, a hot drink will do you a world of good. Unless you'd rather have some lunch first?"

"No, thank you. I'm not very hungry." She couldn't do more than go along with the tide as Mae seemed to conjure up a china teapot and two cups along with a plate of decorated sugar cookies. She wasn't surprised that the teapot was shaped like Santa Claus, with his white-mittened hand as the spout and his tasseled cap as the lid. Thank goodness the cups were just plain red with gold trim. "This is a very unusual teapot," she murmured, running her fingers over the heated porcelain.

Mae beamed. "Thank you, dear. It's been in the family for ages. My Hollis said it went well with his family's dessert dishes that have a similar pattern. I used to say that's why he married me—for my teapot and cups!''

"How long have you and your husband been married?" Quinn ventured, cautiously sipping her tea, relaxing when she discovered it was an orange spice blend.

"Oh, a very long time. Longer than you've been on this earth. Although, we always feel as if each day is our first." Mae poured herself a cup of tea and took the chair next to Quinn. "Now tell me, what do you think of our little village?"

"I never knew this town was even here." Quinn selected a snowman-shaped cookie and bit into it, pleased to find it thick and chewy, just the way she liked them. "Since you're so far out of the way I would think that tourism would have to be your main source of income. I'm not trying to be nosy. It's just that I work in advertising and it's difficult to see how a town could survive this far away from anything but the ski lodge. I would imagine those employees are only hired on a seasonal basis. Do the residents find enough work here in town?"

"We do quite well." She smiled serenely. "We have few needs. And even fewer worries."

Quinn continued sipping her tea, allowing the warm liquid to thaw her cold bones. She nodded when Mae held up the teapot, silently asking if she'd like more tea. "I'll be honest. I naturally assumed this would be peppermint tea."

Mae wrinkled her nose. She leaned forward. "I wouldn't want this to get out, but I'm not all that fond of peppermint," she whispered. "I don't even like candy canes. I prefer horehound, myself."

"Don't worry, I'll keep your secret," she whispered back with a faint giggle. "I know what it was like when I worked on a campaign for a new kind of frozen pizza. I hated the product. It tasted like cardboard, but I had to come up with a way to tell people how wonderful it was."

Mae tsked. "Frozen foods, microwaves cooking complete meals, freeze-dried packets you just add water to. It's disgraceful what's happened in this world over the years. I admit it's a vast improvement over cooking in a fireplace, but at the rate they're going, in the future we'll be eating pills for dinner instead of food."

"That would sure put Julia Child out of business, wouldn't it?" Quinn laughed, taking another cookie— this time a green-frosted tree decorated with tiny silver balls. "Can you imagine turning this into a pill?" She wrinkled her nose. "What an awful thought!"

The two women laughed.

"You still haven't told me what you think of Mistletoe," Mae delicately inquired.

"I'll probably sound like a cliché, but I find it very charming. I just never knew I could find so much holiday cheer in one place. I found some shops just calling out for my credit card."

"Your friend must be enjoying himself if he hasn't come in yet. And I admit it's a bit nippier today than usual."

Quinn ignored Mae's speculative glance. "He's from Southern California, so he's not used to being around snow twenty-four hours a day. You know how men are with new experiences."

Mae picked up her teacup. She paused long enough to select a snowflake cookie. "I'm surprised you'd allow someone so good-looking to wander around alone. We have some lovely single girls here who would snap him up in a reindeer second. He has very passionate hands," she confided. "They're just like my Hollis's hands."

Quinn could feel her face burning with the memory that Santee's hands were most definitely passionate. A memory she wouldn't mind repeating. She hurriedly buried her nose in her cup.

"As I said, we really don't know each other. I met him for the first time yesterday when I picked him up next to his car."

"Dear, it doesn't matter how long you know a person. It's how well."

"Mrs. Berry, you're sounding as if you're trying to play matchmaker. I didn't think that was one of the duties of Santa Claus's helper," she teased.

"We all have our favorite causes and young love is mine. I am a very strong supporter of couples." She wasn't fazed by the playful accusation. "No one should be alone. Especially during the holidays."

Quinn thought of her parents jetting off to island hideaways without giving a thought to their daughter. "Actually, some people prefer to be alone then."

"Only those who want to hide from themselves by flying off to a tropical island where they won't have to listen to Christmas carols or see decorated trees everywhere they turn. They assume they've made so many mistakes with their lives, they don't feel they have a chance to find what they really want."

Quinn's head snapped up. "Tropical islands?" she whispered, the sounds a mere rasp from the bottom of her throat.

Mae smiled. "A hot sun and a bikini don't give a body the holiday feeling, do they?"

Stunned by the woman's words, she slowly shook her head.

Mae glanced up when the clock chimed. "Oh dear, I must see if the dinner preparations have been started. It always seems as if we've just cleaned up the kitchen for lunch and we have to begin on dinner." She stood up and paused to pat Quinn's hand. "You really must relax more and listen to what your heart is saying. And listen to what's going on around you. Don't make any hasty decisions or make them for the wrong reason, dear. Otherwise, you could end up as unhappy as your parents. And we both know, deep down, you don't want that. And you certainly don't deserve it." Before Quinn could recover her wits and question her further, the older woman had bustled off.

"How did she know?" she whispered, staring at the woman's red-aproned back.

"Know what?"

She turned her head. Santee walked into the parlor and dropped into the chair Mae had just vacated. His hair was dark from melting snowflakes.

"According to a very talkative sheriff's deputy, the road crew hasn't had a chance to move the tree yet," he said without preamble as he unzipped his parka. "It's a pretty low priority item since there have been a lot of cars stranded on the highway and a large number of accidents to clean up after." He picked up a cookie and bit into it. He gestured to the pot. "This is good. Is that coffee?"

She shook her head. "Orange spice tea."

He made a face. "No thanks. I don't drink colored water."

"It's not bad. In fact, it's very soothing." She continued drinking just to make her point. "A perfect accompaniment to the cookies you're enjoying so much."

Santee paused, his mouth still open with a cookie on its way in. "I deserve this cookie. While you've been in here playing lady of the manor and taking it easy, I've been out there busting my butt."

Her eyes narrowed with suspicion. "Doing what?"

Santee popped the last of his cookie into his mouth, chewed and swallowed before answering. "I want you to know I helped catch a cute little reindeer named

Vixen. And she was rightly named, too. Talk about a flirt. She sure knew how to tease us guys.''

Quinn rolled her eyes. ''Yeah, right.''

He studied the plate at length before he selected another cookie. ''Scout's honor. I never knew how much trouble an animal could cause until I helped some men chase her down the street. After that, I think I'd rather chase down a suspect. I'd rather face a gun than antlers.'' He raised his shoulder, wincing as a sore muscle made itself known. ''I'm too old to run all over town like that.''

''You're too old to chase after a reindeer, but you weren't thinking twice about spending the next two weeks skiing? Perhaps this was a warning that you need to slow down and take it easy from now on.'' She couldn't resist tweaking the monster named Santee's ego.

His scowl threatened dire consequences, but she wasn't the least bit intimidated. ''There's a big difference. When you ski, you're in control. When you're chasing a damn reindeer, he's the one who's in charge.'' He stood up, pausing long enough to grab a couple of cookies. ''I think I'll go upstairs and take a hot shower.''

''Wait a minute, I planned on eating that tree next!'' Quinn protested.

Santee halted midbite. His teeth came down, neatly severing the top of the tree off. He then quickly twisted the cookie around and placed it between Quinn's lips. She instinctively clamped down on the treat.

"Enjoy," he whispered, rubbing his toe along the length of her foot before ambling off toward the hallway. A moment later, she heard him making his way up the stairs and the faint rumbling of his voice as he greeted someone along the way.

She could taste the sugary cookie interspersed with its faint hint of almond on her tongue. Along with the sweet, she imagined a darker taste left behind by the man who'd tasted it first. She suddenly experienced a mental glimpse of him in the shower. She could swear she was having a hot flash.

"I should have stayed home."

"THE CHILDREN ARE putting on their Christmas pageant this evening in the town hall and we would like to invite all of you to attend," Mae announced to her guests that evening as she made her way through the dining room. "It begins at seven-thirty and we're serving cookies and punch afterward."

"Spare me from small-town entertainment," Clarissa muttered into her coffee.

Quinn, sitting at the adjoining table, shot her a dark look. "It sounds wonderful to me," she said firmly.

"I have a nephew who always sings two bars behind everyone else and he either doesn't notice or he just doesn't care. We're not sure which," Santee commented. "The thing is, he's so enthusiastic when he sings that no one has the heart to discourage him. Not even his teachers."

"Considering I'm tone-deaf, I've always been asked not to sing," Quinn said, savoring her dessert of warm gingerbread topped with french vanilla ice cream and warm caramel topping. She dipped her spoon filled with a small wedge of gingerbread into the ice cream and caramel and swirled it around before bringing it to her lips. She closed her eyes and murmured her appreciation as she rolled the flavors around her mouth. She quickly fixed herself a second bite. As she lifted the spoon toward her mouth, Santee's hand circled her wrist and slowly turned her hand toward him. Keeping his eyes on her startled expression, he steered the spoon into his mouth.

"It's interesting to see what can get you all hot and bothered," he murmured after he'd swallowed his bite. "Spicy, warm, soothing. Appropriate."

"I—" Whatever she was going to say shot right out of her head. She decided she was probably better off that it had. She should remember that she, who makes a living with words, can't even think of a simple statement around this man!

"Get your own dessert," she finally said. Not unique, not even original, but just saying it made her feel better.

"I'd rather share yours." He flashed every watt of his sex appeal at her.

"I don't like to share."

"That comes from growing up an only child. Don't worry, I'll show you how it's done. Trust me, you'll enjoy it." He kept his fingers around her wrist as he guided her hand back to the dish for another bite and directed this one toward Quinn's mouth. She either had to open her mouth or fear the spoon being crammed against her lips. "Sharing can be a lot of fun."

"You two are such a darling couple." Edna giggled as she refilled their coffee cups.

"Oh, yes, he's a real winner, all right," Quinn said sardonically. "Perhaps you could bring him his own dish of gingerbread, so he'll leave mine alone."

"Don't worry about it, Edna. I only wanted a few bites of Quinn's." Santee looked up at the waitress and flashed her his mind-stealing grin.

"All right, but if you want some, just holler. Enjoy the pageant. The kids are just wonderful," she told them before she hurried off to one of the other tables.

"I didn't think a big-city girl like you would enjoy the idea of attending a small-town function." Santee had taken pity on her and was leaving her dessert alone.

"I'm not a complete snob, Santee," she retorted, stung by his assumption. "I enjoy going to a fair or roaming through a flea market just as much as I enjoy going to the ballet or attending the opera."

A corner of his mouth lifted. "Silk and denim. I've always heard it's an interesting combination. I guess you're proof of that."

"Let's get back to other pursuits, shall we?" She hurriedly took possession of the last bite of gingerbread before Santee changed his mind.

"So, you want to go to the pageant with me?"

"Will you behave?" she asked.

"We're talking about sitting with proud parents and grandparents while watching kids meet Frosty the Snowman or invade Santa's workshop. There isn't anyplace you could be safer." He paused for half a beat. "For now."

Quinn felt that familiar heat settling in her chest. She tried to combat this strong attraction to Santee by conjuring up Alan's features, but all she got was a misty image of sandy-blond hair and light blue eyes. She swallowed a boulder-size lump in her throat.

"I think I'll go upstairs and freshen up before we leave," she murmured, carefully setting her spoon by the bowl.

Santee nodded as he watched her stand up and walk out of the room.

"Take my advice," Edna said as she stopped by their table. "Grab that lady."

He grinned, pleased to hear someone was on his side. "I'll do my best."

QUINN LOOKED OUT her window and shuddered at the gently falling snowflakes.

"Definitely dress warmly, Quinn." She searched through her suitcase, lamenting the fact that she'd kept her clothes packed instead of shaking them out and hanging them up. In the back of her mind, she kept expecting to get word the fallen tree was moved and she could leave for Crystal Falls. Surprisingly, the prospect of leaving wasn't as strong as it had been that morning. She began to feel as if there was a reason for her being here. And if so, then Santee was supposed to be here, too.

After she pulled out a sweater and wool pants, she found herself shaking out clothing, hanging things up in the closet and putting lingerie away in the small chest of drawers.

After changing her clothes and redoing her makeup, she returned downstairs where she found Santee in the parlor talking to Clarissa's husband. He stood up when he spied her approaching them.

"Quinn, this is Andrew Chalmers."

The older man smiled as he held out his hand. "I'm the harmless one in the family," he explained. "I also wanted to explain that Clarissa isn't usually this rude. I'm afraid it's been a difficult time for us."

"Because of your granddaughter?" Quinn asked.

Andrew winced at her blunt words. "Clarissa prefers to keep things to herself no matter who it might hurt. It's difficult to explain to a six-year-old child that she can't be with her mother because she needs to be hospitalized for some time." His eyes grew hazy with sorrow. "So Clarissa says nothing and Alice has turned into a very unhappy and confused little girl."

"It sounds as if she has a very understanding grandfather," Quinn said quietly. "That should help."

"I'd like to think it will. I'm just glad she's enjoying herself here," Andrew replied.

"It's a town meant for children and for the child in the adult," Santee commented. "Doesn't seem so bad when you think about it that way, does it?"

Andrew slowly rose to his feet. "I just want you to know that Clarissa really isn't the—" He frowned, trying to come up with the proper word.

Quinn instantly thought of a few descriptions but was polite enough to keep quiet. "We understand," she assured him. "And I promise to take it easy on her."

"Oh, no, I enjoy watching someone who's not afraid to stand up to her," he said. "Most people are intimidated by her imperious manner. Well, I believe I've said too much. Good night." He took his leave.

"That was a surprise." Quinn dropped into the chair Andrew had just vacated. "Does it make you think of 'bad cop, good cop'?"

Santee shook his head. "Not really. You have to put them side by side to get the full effect." He leisurely looked her over from head to toe. "You look very nice."

"I'll be warm and that's what counts." She fiddled with her silver-gray sweater's shawl collar. A deep blue sapphire on a silver chain lay nestled in the hollow of her throat, and matching earrings winked from her earlobes.

"You have a thing about being warm?"

"Not a *thing*. It's a concern, and I'm perfectly willing to admit it. While I love living on the East Coast, I hate the cold, so I do my best to dress as warmly as possible." She glanced at her watch. "How far is the town hall from here?"

"I asked Mrs. Berry. It's about two blocks over. She said it's faster and more convenient to walk there than drive over and have to find a parking place."

Quinn slipped on her coat and draped a scarf around her neck as they headed for the door. Mae was at the other end of the hall wearing a bright red down coat that left her looking like a plump smiling doll. She smiled and wiggled her fingers in a wave.

"I'll see you there," she chirped.

"You're really enjoying all of this, aren't you?" Quinn accused as they walked down the brightly lit sidewalk.

"I told you, I just go with the flow. The fallen tree was beyond our control, so I figure I may as well take in the new experience I've been offered since I never know when I'll learn something I can use later on. Plus, Christmas has always been one of my favorite seasons."

"Then I still can't understand why you're here so far from your family."

He jammed his hands in his pants' pockets as they walked. "I decided I needed a change of scenery for a while."

"Because of your work or because of a person?" she ventured.

"The work doesn't change all that much. I round up the bad guys and put them in jail, and unfortunately, a lawyer usually gets them out."

"So it was some*one* who sent you across the country." She wondered what kind of woman had made him want to leave the state. It must have been a serious relationship for him to go to such lengths. She couldn't imagine any woman giving up Santee without a fight. "You must really be hurting."

"Not as much as I probably should." He grimaced. "I guess because, deep down, we both knew it wasn't going anywhere, but neither one of us wanted to admit it. So, it pretty much died a natural death."

"You didn't do this by letter or over the telephone, did you?"

"Actually, she decided it was either go forward or else. The necklace I gave her for Christmas didn't qualify."

She thought about what he said. "Being a woman and therefore, automatically assuming you, as the male, were in the wrong, I would like to ask if you ever gave her the impression you two had a future?"

"Is that any of your business?"

"It's not," she said, unperturbed by his anger. She stopped to look in a shop window. She stared at his image reflected in the glass. "But that doesn't stop me from asking. Just as it's never stopped you from sticking your nose in my business. So, did you feed her a line, or what? Did she cause a scene? Did you?"

Santee scowled at her reflection. "Why are you so interested in my past love life?"

"Maybe because I'd like to know if it's all in the past." Her whispered words traveled in the frosty air.

He moved until he stood directly behind her with his hands resting on her shoulders.

"It's passed, finished, over, done with. She's going to look for someone who has 'a normal job and lives a normal life,' and I decided it was a good time to get away and figure a few things out, myself."

"Such as?"

"Such as if I'm on the rebound or if this is all something completely different."

"And?" She wasn't sure if she'd said the word out loud, but she must have because he answered her.

"I guess we'll just have to find that out for ourselves, won't we?"

Chapter Six

"The last segment in our program is a story written by our own Ron Sinclair called *The Littlest Christmas Tree,*" the pageant director announced in a bright voice. "Our stars will be Joey Tremaine, playing the part of the littlest Christmas tree and Lisa Allen, playing the Christmas angel." She paused for a moment as her eyes swept over the audience. "Mistletoe Children's Playhouse would like to thank you for attending our first performance for the year. After the program, we will be serving refreshments in the rear of the hall and hope you'll stay to enjoy them." She moved off to the side as the dark green curtains slowly lifted.

Quinn leaned over toward Santee to whisper, "This is wonderful, isn't it? And look at him." She inclined her head toward the stage where a small boy walked on wearing a green tree-shaped cloth costume that covered him from head to toe. Tiny glass ornaments hung from his "branches" along with iridescent strands of tinsel that occasionally fell off as he moved around.

He stood in the middle of the stage looking properly forlorn. "Isn't he cute?"

"The king of Christmas trees said I can't be a Christmas tree because I'm too little," he announced in a piping voice that easily carried to the back row. "Wouldn't a little boy or little girl want me as their tree? Why can't I have a home like all my big brother and sister trees have at Christmas? I don't want to have to wait until I grow up to be a big tree." He pushed his lower lip out so far and threw out such a loud wail, the adults chuckled.

A tiny blond-haired girl wearing a spangled, ankle-length, sky blue net dress, silver wings and silver ballet slippers skipped onto the stage and skidded to a stop just before she ran into the tree. She waved her glittery wand so wildly in the air she almost struck the poor little tree in the face, bringing another wave of laughter through the audience as the wand sent a shower of multicolored glitter through the air.

"Do not worry, little tree. I, the Christmas angel, will give you your wish," she said in a too-loud voice that not only echoed through the hall, it seemed to bounce off the walls. While she kept her body facing the tree, she turned her head to speak directly to the audience as if someone were holding up cue cards for her.

"Something tells me her mother told her to be sure and speak up to the audience," Santee whispered in Quinn's ear. "What do you think?"

"She's beyond speaking up and well on her way to screaming. Funny, I never knew angels carried such lethal-looking wands, let alone a wand, period," she whispered back. "Shouldn't she have been called the Christmas fairy?"

He grinned. "Maybe she's a fairy who changes into an angel at the end of the tale."

Quinn cast glances around her, watching the rapt attention on the adults' faces as they gazed at the participants on the stage. A pang of something—sorrow?—struck her as she realized many members of the audience were around her age and that there wasn't any reason that she couldn't have been the mother of one of the children taking part in the program tonight. She wondered what else she missed out on by worrying about her career more than her personal life.

"All I've done is work like crazy to turn the advertising world on its ear," she said under her breath. When Santee looked at her questioningly, she merely shook her head and smiled as she wrapped her jacket more closely around her.

"Cold?" Santee draped an arm around her shoulders.

She shook her head. "Just wondering how they remember the few lines they're given."

"I bet the moms harass their little darlings to repeat their lines again and again and again," he murmured. "That's what my sister has to do when her kids are in a play."

Quinn smiled. As she inhaled, the faint scent of spice filled her senses along with the darker muskier scent of male skin. With it came memories of his kissing her. As the knee-melting sensation flowed through her body, she was glad she was sitting down. Otherwise, she probably would have collapsed in an ungraceful heap. She looked down at her hands, tightly clasped in her lap. She wasn't surprised at the strange tingling where Santee touched her. She stiffened when she felt a feather-light touch at her nape, then relaxed as his fingers gently massaged the taut skin.

"I give you this star, little tree, so people will know you are a real Christmas tree." The angel tapped her wand a little too energetically on top of the tree's head and then attached a gold glittering star to the top.

"She's dangerous with that thing," Quinn murmured, wincing each time the little girl almost hit the boy.

"I'd prefer to stay out of her way," he said in a low voice, rousing himself to clap along with the others as the angel and tree bowed low at the waist. The rest of the participants ran out onto the stage to take their own bows.

As Quinn applauded, she looked around again and realized that she didn't see Clarissa and Alice. She felt a deep pain at the thought that the little girl had missed such a magical evening. Didn't her grandmother realize how important this would be to her? Didn't she care? Quinn's anger burned toward the older woman.

"I've never attended anything like this before," she told him as they stood and made their way down the row of chairs.

"Maybe you didn't attend, but you must have taken part in plays and musicals like this one when you were a kid," Santee said.

Quinn shook her head. "I always chose not to participate."

He was surprised by her answer. "Not participate? But all the kids join in."

"Not me." She forced herself to smile, to act as if it hadn't mattered to her back then. Even though it had, very much. "I usually left school a couple of weeks before the Christmas holidays, so whichever parent I was with could travel to their favorite spot of the moment. If they were both unavailable, I was sent to my grandparents."

He wished he knew what to say. It was clear she'd felt left out as a child. And to think there were years he used to complain about having to go to play rehearsals.

"I guess I've missed out on a lot." She looked around, feeling wistful as she realized she'd missed out on something very important.

"Oh, well, the pageants I was in didn't have a big-bosomed lady singing holiday classics as if they were opera," he mused, looking upward with a mock-reflective frown.

She swept him a teasing glance from her lowered lashes. "How can you say that? I always thought that "Frosty the Snowman" was a classic."

"What did you think of our entertainment?" Mae patted Quinn on the shoulder as she passed them walking up the crowded aisle.

"I never realized how talented children could be until tonight," Quinn admitted. "I really enjoyed it."

"Are you ready for cookies and punch?" Santee leaned down and murmured in her ear.

Quinn shook her head. "I think I maxed out on the cookies this afternoon."

"Oh, I'm glad I helped you out by eating some of them." As they reached the door, Santee stopped her long enough to zip up her jacket and drape her scarf around her throat. "I feel as if I'm wrapping you up," he said chuckling. As he adjusted the scarf, his fingers grazed her throat, the touch sending a fiery path along her nerve endings. His head shot up when Quinn inhaled a sharp breath. "Careful, lady, or I might be tempted to do a little *un*wrapping, instead," he said under his breath as he ushered her outside.

Quinn stood outside the door, lifting her head to gaze at the stars as she breathed in the crisp cold air, hoping it would help clear her muddled brain.

"I'd say this is more effective than a cold shower." Santee pulled his gloves on before taking Quinn's hand and tucking it into his jacket pocket with his hand wrapped around hers. He paused. "Maybe we should go back inside and see if we can find ourselves a dark corner.''

"If you keep this up, I am going back inside and borrowing that angel's wand to whack over your hard head!" Quinn laughed, pulling on his free hand. She realized how easy it was to respond to his teasing.

He quickly turned his fingers until they encircled her wrist. With a flick of his wrist he brought her up flush against his body. "This is just to show you that we cops have quick reflexes and will not allow dangerous persons to cause harm onto our own persons." The muted light from the street lamp overhead highlighted his dark, dancing eyes.

She arched an eyebrow. "Now what makes you think little old me could bring harm onto your big bad person?" She deliberately exaggerated each word as she tilted her head back. With her eyes sparkling with amusement and lips slightly parted, she was the picture of provocation.

"Probably because you've been dangerous to my peace of mind since that first second I climbed into your car and we laid eyes on each other."

Their surroundings seemed to turn into a foggy haze as they locked eyes. Quinn's lips parted even more, short puffs of fog exhaled with each breath as she focused on his jaw. She wondered what it would feel like to caress the strong line with her fingertips. She usually hated being outside on a chilly night and always complained about her cold extremities, but all she felt now was utter warmth. And the more she looked at Santee, the warmer she grew by the second.

Unable to resist her silent invitation, Santee bent his head and planted a hard kiss on her lips. "Something tells me this G-rated town might not be ready for what I have in mind, sweetheart." He swung around, making sure she was beside him. His steps were so rapid she almost had to run to keep up with him.

"Are we in a hurry to go somewhere?" she panted, finally disentangling her hand from his pocket so she could stop and catch her breath.

He slanted a look at her. "Would it bother you if we were?"

Quinn opened her mouth to question Santee's statement until his exact meaning hit her like a ton of bricks. "Oh," she said very softly, but obviously not softly enough because he had no problem hearing her.

"Yeah, oh."

When they reached the inn, Santee followed her inside. Quinn was never so aware of a man as she was then. She remembered the kiss that had left her lips stinging from the cold combined with the damp heat of his mouth.

"I guess it was being out in all that fresh air that's made me so tired," she said, trying to suppress the memory.

"That can do it."

She ran her hand up the polished bannister as they made their way upstairs. She stopped once and leaned down to sniff the wood. She murmured her delight at the comforting aroma of cinnamon spice instead of the usual lemon oil she associated with furniture polish. When she lifted her head, she was captured by Santee's heated gaze.

Invite me into your room, his eyes said.

It's too soon, her eyes returned.

Quinn turned away before she lost her nerve, continued up the stairs and bid him a chaste good-night at her door.

Once in her room, she changed into her pajamas and socks. Too restless to read or try to sleep at such an early hour, she turned on the small television set, flipping through channels hoping she could find a program that would hold her attention or put her to sleep. But she doubted she would be able to sleep for some time. She felt as if she'd drunk too much coffee. She settled back under the covers and continued to flip through channels.

"I don't remember ever seeing this," she commented to herself as she put down the remote control and settled for watching a movie.

As time passed, Quinn fell under the spell of the love story set during the Christmas holidays. She didn't recognize the actor and actress playing the main characters, but there was no denying the sensual tension vibrating between them. They both had a reason to want to ignore the season of joy but were unable to, thanks to the help of others who knew just how right for each other they were. The more empathy Quinn felt for the lovers as the story unfolded, the harder she chewed on her fingernail. It was so easy to visualize herself and Santee in the leading roles. Santee making love to her. Santee looking at her as if she was a cherished part of his life. The more explicit her visualization became, the more she tried to shake it off. But she couldn't.

"Oh damn!" She looked down at her index fingernail hanging by a thread. She hopped off the bed and ran into the bathroom. "I know I brought it with me," she mumbled, holding her injured finger out of the way as she rummaged through her cosmetics bag. Unable to find the small plastic vial, she finally swore pungently under her breath and picked up the bag and upended it. She swore again as the items scattered across the counter and rolled onto the floor.

"Are you sure you weren't in the marines?"

Quinn spun around. "What are you doing in here?"

Santee rested his shoulder against the open doorway that led to the other bedroom. Just beyond him, Quinn could see his sweater thrown across the end of the bed and the covers a bit rumpled. He'd rolled up his shirtsleeves and left several of the top buttons undone. He looked so much like the man in the movie she was watching that it took a minute to reconcile the film with reality.

"I—ah—I broke a nail and I was trying to find my nail glue," she stammered, dropping to her knees to gather up her cosmetics.

He dropped to one knee and reached out, grasping a small green bottle that rested against the cabinet. "Is this what you're looking for?" He held it up.

She could feel the red creeping up her throat. "Yes." She snatched it out of his fingers and rapidly jumped to her feet.

"You're welcome." Amusement lightened his words.

"It takes me forever to get my nails just the length I want them." Quinn quickly, and carefully, removed her nail polish before fixing the partially torn nail.

Santee wrinkled his nose at the acrid aroma of nail polish remover as he straightened up. "You women use the most godawful-smelling stuff." He looked over her shoulder, watching her as she worked with the delicacy of a surgeon. "So that's how you do it." He turned back to picking up various compacts and makeup brushes. "No wonder makeup bags are so heavy. You carry everything but the kitchen sink in them."

"Ha, ha, very funny." Keeping her repaired nail out of harm's way, she took the items out of his hands. She gasped and snatched her birth control pill container out of his cupped hands. As Quinn turned back around, she caught a glimpse of herself in the mirror and groaned. "No, please tell me no!"

"No, what?"

Quinn stared at her hair—rumpled on one side and slightly flat on the other. She'd washed her face after she'd changed into her pajamas, so there wasn't a speck of makeup on her skin. And most especially her pajamas, her decidedly unsexy hot-pink, turquoise-and-black-plaid flannel pajamas, purchased with warmth and comfort in mind instead of seduction.

"Go away, I look awful," she moaned, gripping the counter with her fingers. "No man should see me looking this horrible."

Santee shook his head, puzzled by her reaction. "You don't look bad. Actually, you look cute." He could tell right away his attempt to make her feel better didn't help.

"Cute, just what a woman wants to hear! Why does a man think telling a woman she looks cute makes it all better?" She lowered her head, pretending to examine her repaired nail. "Why not just tell me I look like an old hag or like something the cat dragged in? Better yet, why not just take me out and shoot me, instead?"

"You're making it much worse than it really is. Come on, take a look." He grasped her shoulders and forced her to look up. "Your skin is clear and glowing, your hair looks sleep-tousled and those pajamas could be considered sexy as hell." His voice dropped an octave.

"Flannel pj's are not sexy."

"Oh?" He slid his hands under the collar of her top, folding it upward until it framed her face. When he felt it didn't look right, he reached down in front of her and slipped two buttons loose, which widened the neckline until the V displayed the shadowy cleft between her breasts. "See." His husky voice washed over her like warm rain.

Quinn was hypnotized by the change she saw in her reflection. The hot-pink collar on her pajama top gave her usually pale face a pleasing rose color and even added color to her lips. Her eyes glittered with tawny lights that left them looking deep and mysterious. Santee's hands still rested on her shoulders, his fingers dark against the pink fabric, all but the two fingers that caressed her bare skin.

"This is how you should look all the time," he whispered, stroking her skin with his fingertips. She shivered with delight under his teasing touch. "All sleep-warm with that just-out-of-bed look."

She unconsciously licked her lips. "I wasn't sleeping. I was watching a movie on channel ten."

He continued moving his fingers in a slow circular pattern, talking to her reflection in the mirror. "What was it about?" His low voice coaxed a reply.

If Quinn had had her senses about her, she would have realized what a crazy conversation they were having, and in the bathroom, no less. But right now, all she could think about was the way his slightly callused fingers felt on her bare skin and how they'd feel if they roamed *all* over her body. Along with the faint idea that maybe flannel pajamas weren't so unsexy, after all!

"It was set during the Christmas holidays," she said huskily as she scanned her memory.

"Sounds about right for where we are." His lips passed over her hair. "And?"

"The couple didn't want to want each other." She blinked to restore her blurring vision.

"Who were they?" He nibbled lightly on her ear.

"Her name was Erin." Her voice was nothing more than a breath. "His was Craig."

Santee nodded. "You wear a very interesting perfume," he murmured, nuzzling her ear. "So what did Erin and Craig do if they didn't want each other?" One hand trailed down her side, coming to rest just below her breast. He cupped the sweet weight in his palm while his other hand slid along her nape, his fingers slowly rubbing the silky skin.

Her head flopped backward against his chest. She closed her eyes as the heat traveled through her body. "The movie hasn't ended yet, but it seems as if they don't have any choice but to get together—as if it's meant to be."

"Sounds like fate—like when you picked me up on the highway, doesn't it?" His breath was warm on her ear.

"It was more an act of kindness with the blizzard getting worse." She felt boneless, as if she'd just had a massage. She tipped her head to one side as his teeth nipped the sensitive skin at her neck. Her voice came out breathless. "Maybe I should go in and find out how the movie does end."

Santee spun her around in his arms. "Why?" He laced his fingers together at the base of her spine so that her lower body rocked easily against his.

"Because..." She frantically racked her brain for a logical answer. "Because I just think it's a good idea."

He smiled and shook his head. "Are you sure?"

She flattened her palms against his chest, resisting the urge to stroke it and discover how his skin felt. "It's all happening too fast, Santee, and if you're not going to tell me your first name, well..." Her voice trailed off. She reluctantly pushed herself out of his arms. She was relieved that he didn't try to detain her. Making sure she didn't look at his face for fear she would weaken, she quickly walked out.

Santee shifted his weight, swearing under his breath as his rock-hard arousal reminded him what he wanted. He wearily rubbed his hands over his face and immediately inhaled the scent of her skin.

He returned to his room and dropped into the chair by the window. Using the remote control to turn on the TV, he found the channel Quinn had mentioned. He frowned at the colorful picture of Daffy Duck racing across the snow to hide a turkey in a snowman. He walked back into the bathroom and knocked softly on the connecting door.

"Quinn? What channel did you say is showing that movie you're watching?"

"Channel ten and it's still on," was her muffled reply that sounded suspiciously as if she was crying.

"And no, you can't come in and watch it with me. This kind of movie always make me cry and I look even worse when I cry than when my hair is mussed up."

Baffled, Santee returned to his room and double-checked the channel—it was on ten. Daffy Duck was back to building a snowman, lisping a holiday carol. He flipped through the various channels and still couldn't find anything close to the movie Quinn had talked about.

"You'd think somebody was broadcasting something entirely different to her."

SNIFFING INTO a tissue, Quinn sat huddled under the comforter watching Erin and Craig finally admit staying away from each other would only bring them more unhappiness.

She blew her nose and blindly groped for another tissue. She used the remote control to flip through the channels and soon discovered another movie that immediately caught her attention. She settled back with the box of tissues in her lap because she expected she'd need them with this film, too. She wondered if Santee had watched the film and how he'd felt when the lovers were finally reunited on Christmas Eve and Craig had asked Erin to marry him so they could spend the rest of their lives together. Did he cry at movies? Probably not. Quinn wondered just what it would take to move Santee to tears.

Chapter Seven

After their encounter in the bathroom the night before, Quinn wasn't about to take the chance of having Santee walk in on her again. Before she even turned on the shower, she made sure the connecting door leading to his room was securely locked. Only then did she feel comfortable enough to shower and shampoo her hair. While she stood under the hot shower, she continually reminded herself he wouldn't just walk in here. Not without her invitation. An invitation she knew would be too easy to offer.

"I shouldn't have stayed up to watch that second movie," she said, sighing and slowly twisting her neck from side to side to relieve the stiffness. Her eyes felt gritty from lack of sleep, and an overall lethargy was threatening to take over at any moment.

When she went downstairs, she found Santee seated at one of the tables in the dining room. With a cup of coffee in one hand and the newspaper in the other, he looked extremely comfortable. He looked up with a smile while he put the paper to one side and half stood as she sat in the chair across from him.

"Good morning." His husky voice sent her nerve endings quivering again.

Damn him, he was acting as if nothing had happened!

"Morning," she murmured, giving Edna a brief smile as the waitress placed a cup in front of her and filled it with coffee.

"French toast, belgian waffle or spanish omelet with hash browns and toast?"

"Edna told me earlier it's their international day," Santee told Quinn.

"Could I just have a couple slices of wheat toast, please?" Quinn requested.

"That's not a very filling breakfast," the waitress protested.

"I'm not used to eating a lot for breakfast and I'd rather not get in the habit."

Edna shrugged and moved off.

"Just because you're ticked off at me doesn't mean you have to take it out on Edna."

His quietly spoken words hit a nerve. She slowly raised her head and gave him a laser-hot look that should have cut him to the bone. "I am not ticked off at anyone, especially you, and I wouldn't dream of taking my temper out on an innocent person." Her sudden smile, instead of turning him into an icicle the way she wanted it to, upped the temperature around them a good fifty degrees and Santee's internal thermometer at least eighty. She turned and flashed Edna the same smile when the woman set a plate of buttered toast and bowl of jam in front of her.

"I still say that's not a proper meal to start the day," the waitress scolded Quinn before she turned away. She gave the younger woman a pointed look as she carefully set a glass of juice on the table.

Santee chuckled at Quinn's expression of disbelief. "I'd say she did an excellent job of getting in the last word."

"How did I get to be so lucky? I usually get waitresses who ignore me when I only want a cup of coffee." She sighed, picked up the glass of juice and drained the contents before setting it back down. "I hope she'll be happy she got her way." She wrinkled her nose. "I hate tomato juice."

He ducked his head to hide his grin. "You're a regular softie, Quinn."

Quinn pulled in a deep breath, looking around almost frantically as if in search of a safety line. When her gaze fell on Mae, a look of relief crossed her face.

"Mrs. Berry!" she called out a bit too enthusiastically.

Santee shook his head, showing disappointment mixed with frustration. "Running away again, Quinn?" he murmured.

Deliberately ignoring his comment, she smiled brightly as the older woman approached their table. "You look so cheerful this morning, you must have good news for us," she greeted her. "Has that tree been cleared away?"

"No, I'm sorry, they haven't gotten to it yet." Mae's smile offered sympathy. "I can't imagine why it's taking so long. They're usually so prompt, but there was another bad storm last night and now even more of the main roads are closed."

Quinn's smile froze on her lips as her fledgling hope died a nasty death. "Are you sure that's what they said? I looked out my window this morning and the snowfall didn't look all that heavy. It's just that I'm afraid there are people worrying about me."

"What's always been so nice is that this valley is usually protected from the nastier storms." She patted Quinn's shoulder. "If you think it would help, why don't you just call your friends to assure them you're all right."

Quinn nodded. "Yes, that's a good idea. I'll call Alan again, just in case he's tried the lodge and discovered I'm not there yet." She shot Santee a look filled with defiance. "We have a lot to talk about." She was so focused on Santee, she didn't see the slight smile lifting the corners of Mae's lips.

"Yes, you do that, dear," Mae murmured, patting Quinn's shoulder again before moving on.

He settled back in the chair, one arm draped along the back. "You're a pretty stubborn lady, aren't you?"

"Just one who knows her mind." Positive she was right, she dropped her napkin on the table. "Excuse me, I have a call to make. I'd like to reach Alan before he leaves for his office.''

His answering nod was a mockery.

Quinn was grateful no one was using the other phone as she squeezed herself against the wall in the rear of the lobby and recited her calling card number to the operator. She drummed her fingernails on the polished wood surface of the table as she listened to the line ringing three times before it was picked up.

''Hello?''

''Alan?'' She injected a sunny note in her voice. ''I'm so glad I caught you before you left.''

''Quinn?'' A harsh exhalation of air proceeded the rest of his words. ''Where the hell are you?''

Even though he couldn't see her, she reflexively drew back from the fury traveling over the line. She couldn't remember the last time he was even mildly annoyed with her. ''What do you mean where am I? I told you where I was the first time I called.''

''A lot of good that did,'' he snapped. ''I called the lodge four times and they said you hadn't checked in yet. I thought you told me you'd be there the following day.''

''I thought so, too,'' she argued. ''I had no idea it would take so long to move one tree. And I've just learned it still hasn't been moved!''

He went on as if he hadn't heard her. Or he was purposely ignoring what she said. ''Naturally, I got worried and called information for the telephone number of the inn you told me you were staying in.

There's only one problem. There is no Mistletoe Inn listed for the entire state," he rasped. "In fact, none of the operators have ever heard of a town called Mistletoe."

"What are you trying to say, Alan?" She kept her voice dangerously quiet when all she wanted to do was scream at the top of her lungs. She unconsciously touched her stomach as the acid burned its way downward.

"I'm saying I would have hoped you would tell me exactly where you are."

Her finger drumming increased to a staccato with each damning word he uttered. "If I didn't know any better, I would think you were accusing me of lying."

"Quinn, I'm just asking you to tell me where you're staying." He lowered his voice to what she called his therapist's purr. "Please don't hide away like this. I worry about you."

"Alan, I am not hiding out." She bit out each word as if they were bullets. "I called you that first day to tell you about the storm—"

"Ah, yes, the horrifying storm that somehow never made the news down this way. Although they did discuss the excellent skiing conditions at Crystal Falls. What a shame you're missing it."

She looked down at her fingers still drumming. She was positive she was drilling holes into the wood. "All I know is that the road leading to the highway is blocked because of a fallen tree," she rapped out. "I have no reason to hide away, no reason to lie to you.

And everywhere I go in this town, all I see is the name Mistletoe." She picked up a red foil book of matches with Mistletoe Inn stamped on the cover in bright gold and slipped them into her pocket. "In fact, just to ease your suspicious mind, I will bring you proof that Mistletoe exists."

"That is one state of mind I don't entertain. Although, Quinn, it does seem that you're going to rather extreme lengths to prove to me where you are."

"And I would say that you're full of—" She sensed a presence behind her and turned to find Santee standing nearby. She bit down to halt the last word in a tirade that she realized was quickly sounding shrewish. She took a deep breath as she gathered her tattered dignity around her. Then she quickly snapped into the receiver, "That you could even think I would do such a thing tells me a lot about the real you, Alan. Now I can honestly tell myself that you've done an excellent job of hiding your true self from me. No wonder I kept putting you off. I think, deep down, I knew if I married you, I'd probably murder you before we celebrated our first anniversary."

"Quinn, you are sounding unreasonable. Just because you're experiencing a few emotional problems right now—"

"Alan, you are probably a wonderful psychotherapist, but I'm beginning to discover that you make a lousy human being." She quickly hung up.

"Does that mean your so-called engagement's off?"

Quinn took several deep experimental breaths. "Strange."

"What? My question, me or the past man in your life?"

She took several more deep breaths to calm her racing pulse. "For the past few months, every time I talked to Alan, my stomach would go nuts and I popped antacids as if they were candy. I was positive I was getting an ulcer except tests showed there was nothing physiologically wrong with me." She turned around and leaned back against the table with her hands behind her. "This is the first time I didn't feel any of that horrible burning in the pit of my stomach. I don't feel any of the craziness I used to feel."

"And?" he probed.

She felt helpless to describe the lightening in her heart. "And . . . I don't know."

He remained in his watchful stance. "Then I'd say it goes to prove that he wasn't the right man for you."

"And you are?" Quinn threw out the challenge.

"Maybe this time was meant for us to find that out." Noticing the people coming and going through the lobby, he kept his voice low so their conversation wouldn't be overheard.

"Why are you so positive about that?"

His dark eyes bored into hers. "Because I've seen how fate works for others and I've begun to think that maybe now my turn has come. Maybe it's yours, too."

She thought about his words. "You enjoy saying that because you know it makes me crazy."

He still hadn't touched her, but his gaze was potent enough to send her pulse racing. "No, I'm saying it because I'm hoping you'll figure out there's going to be some changes in both our futures."

Quinn looked down at the table where her hand still rested on the surface. She'd finally stopped tapping her nails against the top.

"I'm hyperkinetic at times. I've been known to go three days without sleeping when a campaign is reaching the breaking point. While I don't reason problems to death, I have been known to talk them into a coma and I have a stubborn streak a mile wide," she said finally. "Because I'm an only child, I'm considered selfish at times and it doesn't bother me one bit. I've seen enough divorces to last me a lifetime and I consider the majority of my stepsiblings utter idiots, including Benton, my oldest stepbrother who's with the state prosecutor's office in Ohio. He's so pompous and full of hot air, he should be a balloon. Sybil, my stepsister from my dad's second marriage, lives in a world all her own. Her goal in life is to redecorate her apartment in brightly colored chintz and look for Mr. Right. Last I heard, she was on Mister Right number three. Luckily, the number in my extended family slowed down as Dad's choice in wives got younger and my mother's choice in husbands got older. No wonder I outgrew the Easter Bunny, Tooth Fairy and Santa Claus before all my friends."

Santee wondered if she realized just how much pain she still carried inside. "Then it's time you made some new friends and discovered a whole new world.'' He held out his hand.

She hesitated. She was still smarting over Alan's accusation and wasn't sure it was wise to give in to this man who made her feel all too much. "I didn't get to finish my toast."

"I bet Edna would happily get you fresh hot toast."

Quinn hesitated. Maybe it wouldn't be so bad to walk on a new wild side with him. "I'll want raspberry jam this time."

He nodded.

"And then you'll tell me about these new friends I'm going to make?"

He grinned. "You're a smart lady. I think you'll figure it out pretty quick."

"PLEASE, Gramma, can I?" Alice begged Clarissa as they sat at a table near the dining room's open archway.

Clarissa looked at Mae over the top of the child's head as she formulated an answer.

"She'll be fine," Mae assured her. "Every little girl should make gingerbread cookies once in her lifetime."

"She's so little. She'll probably get in the way and make a horrible mess," Clarissa countered.

"That's what damp sponges are for. Besides, what's cookie-baking without a bit of a mess?" Mae chuckled, her plump body swaying with her laughter. "We love to have children in the kitchen helping us bake the cookies. It makes them feel important." She rested her hands on Alice's shoulders. "Would it be all right?"

Any refusal Clarissa might have given was lost in Mae's soft-spoken request.

"I suppose it would be all right since Alice wants to so badly." She spoke haltingly, looking down at her granddaughter's excited face.

"Thank you, Gramma!" Her heart-shaped face glowed with excitement.

"See, magic can occur here," Santee said quietly as they silently skirted the small group.

"The only magic would be if Mae was that poor child's grandmother and she received some real love," she murmured. The tense expression on her face stopped him from replying.

Quinn decided against the toast, and the two quickly gathered up their coats.

"Don't you think it's surprising that everything we need is within walking distance?" She glanced at her car as they walked past the parking lot.

"Don't worry. I started it up this morning and it's just fine."

"He."

He cocked an eyebrow. "He?"

"Actually, his name is Alvin." She quickly pulled on her gloves.

"You named your car Alvin?"

Quinn nodded. "You know Alvin the chipmunk? It fits the car's personality since he never does what I ask him to do. Don't you have a name for your car?"

"I usually drive an official vehicle and my Jeep is so old, I doubt it's worthy of a name."

"A Jeep?" She pursed her lips in thought as she walked along, momentarily forgetting the cold. "What color?"

"Sort of dark gray with plenty of scratches and dings to give it character. It's well broken in."

"There's no question about it—Patton."

He jumped to one side to evade a little girl rolling more than running in her heavily padded snowsuit. "Patton?"

Quinn stopped to let him catch up. She dug her hands into her parka pockets. "Jeep, scratches and dings, character. He sounds like a Patton."

"What if it had been a Range Rover?"

"W.C."

He found himself more amazed each day by her quick mind. "For Fields or water closet?"

"Neither. Winston Churchill. You're talking about a British-manufactured product, and Elizabeth really wouldn't be a proper name for such a rugged vehicle."

"Do you always name your cars?"

"It makes it easier to kick it when the heater goes out during the winter or the air-conditioning shuts down during the summer," she explained. "And it sounds better when you're swearing at a name instead of an inanimate object. For a while, I had a little car I called Oliver Hardy. If I'd owned a gun, I would have shot it to put us both out of our misery."

"You have an incredible imagination," he said with honest admiration.

"It comes in handy in my line of work."

"Then make sure you rely on it today." Santee pulled her down Jingle Walk, not stopping until they reached a tiny red house with candy canes lining the walkway leading to the front door. "Don't worry, we don't need an appointment."

Ironically, his assurance didn't make her feel better. She began to drag her heels but it didn't make any difference since he barely exerted any strength to tug her along. "That really makes me feel a great deal better. We don't need an appointment? Wait, don't tell me. This is Mistletoe's idea of a police station, right?"

"No, we're just stopping by to see an old friend."

This time, she dug in her heels until he had no choice but to stop. "How can you have an old friend in a town you've never been to or known about until a couple days ago?"

Santee inclined his head until his lips just brushed hers. "I didn't say he was an old friend of mine," he corrected. "Just that he's an old friend. Meaning he's an old friend of mine *and* yours. You'll see what I mean. Trust me."

She exaggerated each word. "I'd sooner trust Alan."

"Mr. Compassionate who hangs on your every word?"

Quinn smiled at his wry observation. "Wouldn't it be easier to just give me a hint as to your old friend's name?"

"You're a smart lady, you'll figure it out soon enough."

"Hello there!" The booming male voice brought Quinn around.

"Naturally, there would be a Santa Claus," she sighed, shooting Santee a dark glare. "For the kiddies."

The man who led them into the house could have been Kris's identical twin. Except this man wore the requisite red suit trimmed with white fur. His polished black boots rivaled a marine's for mirrored shine. The high-backed gold and forest green velvet-covered chair he sat in wasn't as elaborate as some of the chairs she'd seen in the malls, but it seemed to have a great deal more character.

"Actually, Quinn, I'd like to think that I'm here for children and adults alike." Even his deep voice and warm smile was the same as Kris's.

She hung back. There was something about the way his kindly eyes looked into hers that unnerved her. As if he knew more about her than she cared anyone to know. "No, thanks. I stopped sitting on Santa's lap when I was seven. That was when I decided there couldn't be a real Santa Claus. And not just because you could find one in every major department store and mall, but because I didn't want to believe Santa smelled of scotch."

Santa's benign smile sent uncertainty winging its way to Quinn's soul.

"You have trouble believing in anything you can't touch or see, don't you, Quinn?"

She shrugged. "It's not that. It's just that I grew up. And grown-ups don't believe in that sort of thing."

Santee remained quietly off to one side. His hands in his pockets, he rocked back and forth slightly on his heels as he listened to the conversation. When he first found Santa's cottage the day before, he had a strong feeling he should bring Quinn here. A picture of her looking flushed and unsettled wearing those flannel pajamas crept into his mind. Who would have thought a woman could be so sexy in something like that. But then, Quinn gave a whole new meaning to flannel pajamas and fuzzy socks. Funny, he'd only kissed her a few times, but he already knew it could be easy to fall for her. Now all he had to do was convince her it wouldn't be all that bad to fall for him.

"Why do you dislike Christmas so much, Quinn?" Santa asked in a quiet gentle voice that invited confidences.

His question threw her. "I don't dislike it."

"But you don't look forward to it, either, do you? You don't go shopping and decorate your apartment or even, like many, revert to your childhood awe for the holiday." His bright blue eyes were solemn now instead of twinkling. "Is it because no one allowed you to celebrate it as a child?"

She hadn't felt this uneasy since her one and only trip to the principal's office when she was in the third grade and had hit Tommy Maddox for calling her a booger-face. "Are you sure you're not a psychologist? Or a mind reader?"

He chuckled. "Positive. They're too difficult to deal with. They're always trying to find out why I do what I do. While I would think that was very obvious."

"How many people do you know who enjoy riding in an open sleigh—that probably doesn't even have a foot heater—on a very cold night of the year?" Quinn countered. "Not to mention dropping through a chimney that barely has room for a bird's nest." She glanced pointedly at his roly-poly belly. "It's not a picture I can easily visualize."

Santa threw his head back and laughed. "I don't think I'm going to have to worry about you anymore, Quinn. Whether you care to admit it or not, you see things a great deal more clearly now than you did when you first arrived. In fact, you just might get what you've been asking for for a long time." He reached into a bright red velvet pouch by his chair and pulled out two candy canes. He handed one to Quinn and one to Santee. "Now why don't you two head for the southern edge of town where there's a lovely empty field covered with pristine snow where you can make all the snow angels you want. I believe there's nothing more stimulating than making snow angels, don't you?" He beamed at both of them.

"Very cute, Santee," she chided as they walked outside. She tucked her candy cane into her jacket pocket while he unwrapped his and stuck the straight end into his mouth.

"I never thought of myself as cute, but who am I to argue with an expert?"

Quinn hastened her steps until she could walk backward while facing him. She wanted to see his face while she blasted him to hell and back.

"I'm talking about the obvious setup back there. The way he talked to me as if he already knew me. How he just happened to know my name," she accused, wagging a finger in his face.

He grabbed hold of her wandering finger and wrapped his fingers around her hand, turning her around to walk beside him. "There was no setup, Quinn. I saw the cottage yesterday and thought you'd like to see Santa in his natural habitat, that's all. I didn't even go inside or speak to him."

She still wasn't convinced. "Then how did he know my name?"

Santee shrugged. "It's a small town and it's pretty obvious we're two of the few visitors they have right now. It would be easy enough to figure out."

Quinn nodded. "True," she conceded. A sudden light sparked in her eyes. "Still, if he *is* the real Santa Claus, then he'd have to know your entire name, wouldn't he?" She started to turn around.

GET A FREE TEDDY BEAR...

You'll love this plush, cuddly Teddy Bear, an adorable accessory for your dressing table, bookcase or desk. Measuring 5½″ tall, he's soft and brown and has a bright red ribbon around his neck—he's completely captivating! And he's yours *absolutely free*, when you accept this no-risk offer!

AND FOUR FREE BOOKS!

Here's a chance to get **four free Harlequin American Romance® novels** from the Harlequin Reader Service®—so you can see for yourself that we're like **no ordinary book club!**

We'll send you four free books...but you never have to buy anything or remain a member any longer than you choose. You could even accept the free books and cancel immediately. In that case, you'll owe nothing and be under **no obligation!**

Find out for yourself why thousands of readers enjoy receiving books by mail from the Harlequin Reader Service. They like the **convenience of home delivery**...they like getting the best new novels months before they're available in bookstores...and they love our **discount prices!**

Try us and see! Return this card promptly. We'll send your free books and a free Teddy Bear, under the terms explained on the back. We hope you'll want to remain with the reader service— but the choice is always yours! 154 CIH AK9G (U-H-AR-12/93)

NAME

ADDRESS   APT.

CITY   STATE   ZIP

Offer not valid to current Harlequin American Romance® subscribers. All orders subject to approval.
© 1993 HARLEQUIN ENTERPRISES LIMITED   **Printed in U.S.A.**

NO OBLIGATION TO BUY!

"Forget it, sweetheart." He kept a tight hold on her hand. "Even Santa isn't crazy enough to give out that kind of privileged information."

"Then it must be one horrible name," she mused, eyeing him with a speculative gaze.

"Not horrible, just not me," was all he would say.

As they walked down the sidewalk, Quinn couldn't help thinking about her encounter with Santa Claus. No matter how much she might argue with Santee about that famous man in the red suit, she couldn't help but sense there was more to Santa than met the eye. Santee's glib explanation of how Santa knew her name was very believable and certainly plausible. So why did she have trouble believing his explanation? Why was she rolling it over in her mind so much when it really shouldn't matter? Why did she feel as if she needed to learn the truth.

Deep down, she had a feeling her disbelief in Santa's knowledge just might have something to do with the niggling thought that some sort of magic told him that, for the first time in years, she'd actually made a Christmas wish.

Chapter Eight

"Do you want to let me in on the secret behind making snow angels?" Santee asked. This question hung in the air as they walked down the sidewalk toward the edge of town. Soon, they came to a field where there were only broad stretches of pristine snow on either side of them. "About the only thing I know to do with snow is start snowball fights."

Quinn grabbed hold of the back of his ski parka and jerked him to a stop. "I guess snow angels would be considered more a girl thing than a guy thing," she agreed as she urged him toward the side of the road where a tall drift of snow spilled out onto the road. "Turn around so you're standing with your back to the snow," she said crisply, holding on to his shoulders and adjusting his position until she was certain he stood right where she wanted him.

He remained still with his arms held stiffly at his sides. "What are you doing?" he asked, wary of her intentions.

Quinn moved until her breasts lightly brushed against his chest. Even with the heavy material separating them, she could feel the electricity between them. "Just relax because you're going to love this." The tip of her tongue just barely appeared between her slightly parted lips. The lipstick she'd put on that morning seemed to glow against the soft pink skin. Santee's body started to lean in her direction, but her fingers against his chest tipped him back upright.

"And now to show you the magic behind snow angels," she whispered, slowly walking her fingers up his chest. Standing so close to him she could smell the sharp peppermint on his breath from the candy cane he'd just finished, she continued whispering in a provocative tone that brought fire to his gaze. "And the best way to learn about them is to... make one." She splayed her hands across his chest, pausing long enough to savor the feel of hard muscle under her fingertips. She mentally ordered herself to block it out of her mind as she planted her hands flat against his chest. "And to make one, all you have to do is just fall right back into it!" She suddenly laughed as she gave a mighty push that threw him off-balance. Quinn screamed as his arms wrapped around her at the last second so that she fell with him, landing hard on his chest.

"Oof!" he grunted. "You're heavier than I thought." He dropped his head back in the snow.

"That was a dirty trick!" she accused, pounding his chest as she scrambled to sit up.

"If I were you, I wouldn't accuse anyone of dirty tricks." He looked so calm...as if he hadn't just fallen into a very cold mattress of snow. He grasped her waist as she sat up straighter. Could she miss the fact that she was now in a very tantalizing position, with her knees on each side of his hips? "I had no idea a devilish trick could turn into a snow angel."

Quinn, realizing she was well and truly caught, started to shift her weight. As she caught the fire in Santee's gaze, she suddenly realized where she was sitting. And what her position was doing to him. As she tried to move away, his fingers dug into her waist.

"If only it wasn't so damned cold out here and we weren't in a public place where we could be arrested for what I'm thinking of doing. I guess you can't consider snow as soft as a featherbed," he said hoarsely, moving his hands up under her jacket until they rested against the soft wool of her sweater. "What do you think, Quinn? Think we could turn this snow into steam?"

The ground could have opened up and she couldn't have moved. The firm strength of his erection pressed against her as her eyes locked on his.

"This isn't..." As always, where he was concerned, words failed her. Her body wanted to arch up against his, but she tried to keep her brain in control. And her brain was rapidly losing the battle. Her cap tipped forward over one eye, but she didn't seem aware of it. "Why is this happening to us?"

His fingers splayed out until they rested just under her breasts, then traveled farther upward until he could feel her erect nipples. "Fate."

Quinn wanted nothing more than to stretch out on top of Santee and absorb his strength. To find out what made him the man he was, why he caused such a turmoil in her. A turmoil she now realized was an echo of what she caused within him.

"If we tried to kiss each other, our lips would probably freeze together."

He grinned. "It sounds better than getting a handful of snow in the face, doesn't it?"

"It wouldn't be all that pleasant having an emergency team cut us apart." She was extremely careful getting off of him. She stood over him with her hand outstretched.

Santee accepted her assistance, careful not to throw her off-balance as he struggled to his feet. He took several deep breaths to calm his racing blood. He looked down at her upturned face with her flushed cheeks and bright eyes, and found himself falling under her spell again.

"What about that snow angel?"

She heaved a silent sigh, relieved that the intense mood was broken with his teasing comment.

"Oh, that's easy!" She laughed merrily as she dropped onto her back and waved her arms and legs up and down in the snow before carefully getting up.

Santee looked down and saw the impression left in the snow. There was no denying the impression looked very much like an angel. "I think you make a much better angel than I would."

The muted sound of shouting and laughter caught Quinn's attention. She turned around looking for the source.

"Look at them!" She pointed off toward a series of hills where children and adults were pushing off in aluminum saucers or sleds. "Come on, let's go watch." She grabbed his hand and he had no choice but to follow.

They walked over and joined the small crowd of spectators at the bottom of the hill.

"When I was younger, I always loved winter because I could go sledding," Quinn confided to Santee as two girls on a sled screamed past them. "To me, it was better than any roller coaster."

"Then I think we should relive the good stuff." This time, he pulled on her hand as he walked over to the two girls. "Would you mind if we oldies tried it?" he asked them.

Quinn couldn't help but notice the girls were as captivated by his charm as she was.

"Sure you can use it." The older girl handed him the rope. "Our parents use it all the time, so it'll hold you."

"What a comforting thought," he murmured to Quinn as they pulled the sled up the hill. He looked around at the varying degrees of slopes. "So you wanna go for the kiddie slope or tackle an E-ticket ride?"

Quinn looked confused. "E-ticket?"

"It's a throwback to the days when Disneyland issued tickets for the rides, A being the real easy stuff and E being the scary, bumpy rides. E's were always considered the best." He led the way to the steeper hill. "Come on, let's go for it."

"It's not the same as skiing," she warned, watching him line up the sled at the top edge of the slope.

"No, it's not. It's even better. This way I can hold on to you."

Quinn settled herself in front. She looked over the curved top of the sled. It seemed a long way to the bottom. It didn't help her courage any to see someone spill off their sled on the next hill.

"This looks awfully steep," she said hesitantly. "Are you sure...? No, we can't. No, Santee! *No!*" she screamed just as Santee pushed them off and jumped on behind her with his legs stretched out alongside hers. In a split second, he wrapped his arms around her waist, pulling her back into the V of his legs as he took hold of the heavy rope attached to the front.

Quinn's shrill scream echoed through the air as she stared at the ground rushing up at them.

"We're going to crash!" Her wail followed on the heels of her scream.

"No, we're not!" Santee laughed in her ear as the sled picked up speed.

She was so dazed by the increasing speed of the sled as it raced down the hill, she didn't have the nerve to cover her eyes. Before she could gather up enough breath to let loose with another bloodcurdling scream, the sled finally reached the bottom and coasted to a stop.

"Wasn't that great?" Santee jumped to his feet and reached down for Quinn's hand. He grinned as she held on to him with a death grip as she got up on rubbery legs.

"Oh, yeah, it was so much fun I can't imagine why I stopped sledding. Maybe it had something to do with the state of my stomach," she gasped, tightening her grip on his arm as she took in much-needed gulps of air. "I always liked to keep it where it belonged and not in my throat."

"Talk about the thrill of speeding legally." He grinned his thanks as he returned the sled to the two girls. "What's the problem? You love skiing. I thought that was pretty much the same."

She shook her head, then pressed her hand against her rolling stomach. "No, it wasn't. When I'm skiing, I'm not on something that could toss me head over heels."

"No, but you could meet up with another skier who could do it to you. Think they'd let us use the sled again?" He started back toward the girls.

"Give them a thrill and go with them." She stopped in her tracks. "I'll stick with what I can absolutely control."

Santee laughed as he wrapped his arms around her waist and spun her in a circle. "That's your problem, you have to learn there are times when it's okay to lose control," he murmured in her ear. "Besides, you know I wouldn't have let anything happen to you. Here, this will settle your stomach." He reached in her jacket pocket and pulled out her candy cane.

Quinn felt the sharp peppermint taste first freeze, then warm her mouth. And then gradually settle her stomach. "I also don't remember ever sledding down a hill that steep. You were right about the E-ticket ride."

"Come on, Quinn, admit it was fun," he teased as they walked back toward town. His legs were considerably more stable than hers were.

"Fun? I want you to know I don't scream like that when I consider something fun!"

He kept one arm around her waist as he bent his head and whispered in her ear, "Bet I could make you scream while you're having some fun."

Now it wasn't just the winter cold that was turning Quinn's cheeks bright red. It was a few seconds before she could form a coherent thought.

"Honestly, Detective, it's a shame you're so shy about expressing your thoughts. I do hope you'll recover from that horrid affliction." She poked her elbow in his ribs and grimaced as she realized that even with the padded clothing he wore to protect himself against the cold, there was nothing but rock-hard muscle underneath. But that was all right, because for once, she'd had the last word!

"YOU REALLY THINK he's sexy?"

"Yes! They're two great movies. I get a rugged sexy

man in one, and a confident but slightly crazy woman in the other. Two of my favorites." Quinn scrunched down in the upholstered seat and draped her legs over the seat in front of her. She held a large paper cup of diet cola in one hand and several pieces of red licorice in the other.

Santee chuckled as he studied her relaxed position. "Something tells me an afternoon spent at the movies is nothing new to you."

She chomped down on her licorice. "On days when everything goes wrong at the office and a new idea couldn't come to me if my life depended on it, I sneak away from work and head for the movies. Multiple-screen theaters are great for my thought processes. I've been known to work my way through several movies in one day. Often I go home bleary-eyed and sometimes more than a little nauseated from all the popcorn and licorice I've eaten." She made her point by snitching a couple of pieces of popcorn from his container. "It's incredible, they use real butter here. Anyway, I usually come up with at least a germ of an idea from watching a movie."

When they'd passed the movie theater ten minutes earlier after eating lunch, Quinn hadn't hesitated in noting the double feature was starting soon. She suggested it might be a nice warm way to spend the afternoon. Santee thought there might be an even better, warmer way but already knew Quinn wouldn't agree with his idea.

"This is just great," she enthused, lowering her voice the same time the lights dimmed and the red velvet curtain covering the screen slowly ascended. "*A Holiday Affair* with Robert Mitchum and Janet Leigh and *Christmas in Connecticut* with Barbara Stanwyck and Dennis Morgan."

"Personally, I prefer watching Mitchum in his darker films."

"I don't care what the man does. I think he's as sexy in his lighter roles as he is in his darker ones." She chewed on her licorice. "And I've always envied the self-confidence Barbara Stanwyck displays. Men could never get anything past her."

Santee's attention was briefly diverted by the black-and-white titles flashing across the screen. He soon discovered that Quinn was most definitely a serious moviegoer. Her gaze was glued to the screen and didn't waver even as she occasionally sneaked a hand into his popcorn container.

"Get your own," he whispered, lightly slapping her errant hand. "Besides, I thought you only wanted the licorice because you were too full from lunch for popcorn."

"I am, but that doesn't mean I can't steal some from you." She then proved her point by snitching a few more pieces. "Besides, didn't your mother teach you to share?"

"Not when it comes to my popcorn." He grinned as he watched a young Janet Leigh crisply inform toy salesman Robert Mitchum what model train she

wanted to buy. From there, the story turned into a
minor roller-coaster ride with her young son mistak-
enly thinking the train was for him and Janet Leigh's
gentleman friend waiting for her to say yes to his
marriage proposal. But Robert Mitchum always
seemed to show up at just the right time.

"She had to go after him," Quinn sighed during the
ending credits. "No offense to Wendell Corey, but
when a woman can have Mitchum..." She lifted her
shoulders as if that said it all.

"Now, if I remember the next movie correctly, she's
engaged to one man but ends up with another." He
shot her a telling glance. "Kind of makes a statement, doesn't it? You'd almost think it could happen
in real life."

She raised her chin. "I doubt it. We're talking about
fiction here." She stood up. "Now if you'll excuse me,
I'll be back in a moment. And please make sure no one
tall sits in front of my seat." She walked out into the
lobby with her head held high.

"Women sure like to argue, don't they?" A man in
his late twenties smiled down at Santee as he walked up
the aisle.

"They just like to make sure we know who's in
charge," he said sardonically. "If I'm not being too
curious, what does a man your age do around here to
make a living? From what I've heard, there isn't any
industry all that close by."

"I don't mind answering at all. Bakeries always do
an excellent business." He nodded and moved on.

It wasn't until after the man left the theater that Santee realized his question hadn't truly been answered. He turned around and waited for the young man to come back. There was still no sign of him when Quinn returned.

"Don't you think it's strange that they didn't show any previews," she commented, dropping into her seat.

"The locals probably know what's playing here before the theater changes its marquee."

When the second feature began, Quinn shifted around to make herself more comfortable, not surprised to find Santee's hand wrapped around hers.

"Too bad drive-ins are out of style," he murmured.

"Going to a drive-in theater during the winter would be insane."

His lips brushed her ear. "Then call me insane. And believe me, we wouldn't be in a car that had bucket seats."

Quinn was positive the temperature in the theater rose a good fifty degrees. "I think it's a good thing I didn't know you in high school," she murmured, forcing herself to stare at the screen although she couldn't even fathom what was happening between the celluloid characters.

As the story moved along, the similarities stunned her. It was about a self-assured businesswoman who had little idea about domesticity and was involved with a man she talked herself into thinking she was in love

with. It could have been her and Alan! Then the hero,
Dennis Morgan, appears on the scene, calls out to
Barbara Stanwyck's soul and she's a goner from there
on. Just as Quinn was finding herself a goner under
Santee's charm. And he was a sheriff. A man who
wears a uniform. Then, there was the first film.
Working woman already involved with professional
man. Another man comes on the scene at a crucial
point in their relationship. A military man. A man
who once wore a uniform. The more she thought
about it, the more she regretted her suggestion that
they spend the afternoon at the movies.

She had no idea two light comedy films would force
her to start rethinking certain areas of her life. She was
also surprised to realize that, while she didn't like the
holiday season, she had always liked the movies de-
picting that time of year.

Santee was equally quiet as the second film reached
its climax.

When they silently exited the theater, Quinn happened to look down the street and saw Alice standing
in front of the toy store staring into the window. There
was something about her forlorn expression that
struck Quinn's heart and brought faint memories a
little closer to the surface. She had to turn away before she gave in to her emotions and scooped the little
girl up and comforted her, and probably incurred
Clarissa's wrath in the process.

"NONE OF IT makes any sense," Quinn muttered hours later as she paced the length of her bedroom. She had tried to go to sleep more than an hour ago and was unable to do more than lie there and suffer some pretty erotic daydreams starring her and Santee. By now, she had worked herself into such a state she couldn't remain calm. "How can I act like a sexstarved woman when I barely know the man?"

It was easy when the man did such wonderful things to her libido! He knew exactly what buttons to push. She wondered with erotic fascination what it was going to be like to have him as a lover, because, no matter how much she protested, she knew it was inevitable. She wanted to hate him for making her feel this way. She *should* hate him!

As the latter emotion started to build up inside her, fury began to overtake her earlier fascination.

"Damn him!" She picked up one of the bed pillows and threw it across the room. It bounced off the wall and landed on the dressing table. "How can he do this to me!" The second pillow quickly followed the first. "Who does he think he is?"

Tell him how you feel.

She halted her tantrum when a tiny voice uttered the words in her ear.

Go on. Go in there and tell him how angry you are with him.

"Good idea, I think I will," she replied to the gremlin sitting on her shoulder who whispered the mischievous suggestions. She squared her shoulders and marched through the bathroom. She flung open the connecting door without bothering to knock, not even wincing when it hit the wall.

"How dare you!" she accused, walking over to the bed where a surprised-looking Santee lay stretched out with a mystery novel in his hands.

"How dare I?"

"You—you—!" Failing to come up with an appropriate description, she yanked his pillow out from under his head and began hitting him with it. "How dare you make me fall for you!"

Since Santee was too busy shielding his head with his arms, it took a moment for Quinn's words to register. He suddenly looked up, then yelped when the pillow hit him square in the face.

"Hey, watch it!" He curled up under her assault but soon realized he only gave her a more stable target. "Quinn, calm down and tell me what the problem is."

"You're the problem, you cretin!" she shrieked, hitting him again and again with the pillow.

Realizing he was going to have to take some action before she either battered him to death or tore the pillow apart, he rolled out of the bed and onto his feet. With a swift movement, he grabbed hold of the free end of the pillow and jerked it out of her hands. Before she could even try to retrieve it, he tumbled her onto the bed and shackled her wrists with his hands, pulling them down to her sides. When she tried to kick him, he quickly draped one leg over her two. His grin should have been her undoing.

"I made you fall for me?"

Undaunted at being so efficiently taken down, she glared at him, practically spitting out her anger. "Yes, you did and you know it. Don't I have enough problems in my life without having to worry about you, too? I should have let you freeze out on the highway!"

Santee made the biggest mistake he could have made at that moment. He threw his head back and laughed.

"Don't you laugh at me, you cad!" She twisted this way and that to try to loosen his hold on her but her efforts did nothing more than cause further laughter on his part. Her eyes spat out fiery darts that would have killed him had they been real.

"All right," he readily agreed. "Then I'll try something else to cool that hot little temper of yours. Although knowing you, you'll only find another way to fight back."

Quinn's eyes widened as she realized his intent. When his mouth covered hers, any thought she had of killing him drastically changed.

"Go ahead, bite me," he murmured, running his tongue across her lower lip. "That's what you want to do, isn't it? Come on, Quinn, let me feel your teeth sink into my skin, taste me as I taste you." His voice grew raw with arousal.

When she tried to free one of her hands, her fingers brushed against his hip and she got another shock.

She had barged in here, so intent on making him suffer for driving her crazy that she hadn't even thought of what might happen. Now she knew. Along with the knowledge that the man, at the moment, was very aroused.

Santee's expression was faintly amused as he watched the various emotions cross her features.

"When you squirm all over me, you've got to expect something like this to happen. At least I'm wearing my underwear, Quinn. I usually sleep in the raw. So tell me, Quinn, are you thinking you might have gotten a little more than you expected?"

Chapter Nine

"Santee, I want you to let me up right now." Her wide eyes bored into his as she forced herself to speak calmly. "I am not kidding about this. This is not a good idea!"

Her choked-out words, bordering on panic, only broadened his smile.

He arched an eyebrow. "Sweetheart, let me remind you that *you* were the one who barged into my room. *You* were the one who attacked me with my very own pillow, and *you* were the one who ranted and raved at me, heaping accusations on my head that I made you fall for me. All I was doing before your onslaught was lying here innocently reading my book."

"Get off of me." She punctuated each word with dangerous precision as she pressed against his chest. She would have had better luck trying to push a mountain. *"Now."*

Undeterred by the murderous spark in her gaze, he deliberately took his time getting up.

"And put some clothes on!" Her quiet hiss echoed through the room.

Clearly unembarrassed by his near nudity, he sauntered over to the chest of drawers. Quinn turned her head, confident he couldn't see her sneak a peek at what she privately considered one of the best pair of male buns she'd seen in a long time. She pursed her lips in a silent whistle when the muscles in his flanks flexed as he pulled open the top drawer and pulled out a pair of faded navy sweatpants. He leaned over, giving her an even better view. She carefully turned her head back to its original position.

"Get a good enough look or should I ignore your ogling for a few more minutes till you've had your fill?"

Out of the corner of her eye she could see him smiling as he stepped into the pants and pulled them up, tying the drawstring at the waistband. Even then, she noticed they hung loosely on his hips.

"I see you have the same glitter pattern across your ceiling. Except yours is gold and mine is silver," she couldn't resist adding as she raised herself on her elbows and stared at the ceiling. "And, by the way, I don't ogle."

The crooked slant of his mouth told her he took her huffy protest with a grain of salt.

She shot up to a full sitting position and forced herself to face him squarely. She schooled her expression until she was certain it was absolutely blank. At least she hoped it was blank. "I hate to disappoint you, but you don't have anything any other man doesn't have." *Admit it, Quinn, you haven't seen a more appealing package, even in a fashion magazine.* By now, she was ready to strangle that little voice in her brain that had already done more than its share in getting her into trouble! Still, he did have a very nice chest. The kind that was broad enough to be comforting but narrowed down to a washboard belly. The kind that had just the right amount of dark curling hair against bronzed skin. The kind of chest any red-blooded woman wouldn't mind curling up against. And she most definitely had a lot of red blood. And the way that soft fleece fabric draped around his hips as if it might fall down at any moment... An enterprising woman would only need to flick her fingers to tug them down in order to... She gulped.

"I'm sorry I was so rude." She feared she was babbling as she scrambled off the bed. "I have no idea what came over me. It must have been something I ate for dinner. Or maybe PMS is coming early."

"You barely touched your food. And I doubt you ever allowed PMS to rule one day of your life."

"Yes, well, it was probably all that popcorn and licorice I had at the movies. It tends to fill me up. After all, they do say that popcorn is fiber and fiber is considered very filling." Oh, Lord, I'm babbling again, she thought, desperate to get out of his room. "As for the PMS, we women have no control over those ornery little hormones." She started to edge her way toward the connecting door. Then realized that he was standing right in front of it. "I'll be going now. I'm sure you're tired," she said meekly.

His dark eyes softened with understanding. "Quinn."

Further amusement on his part she could have handled. Even derision. But not this. She dropped back onto the bed.

"I don't understand what's going on. Nothing is going the way it was supposed to. The way I planned it," she wailed, throwing her hands up. "I was looking forward to a wonderful vacation skiing. I brought a few books to read in the evenings by the fireplace if I didn't care to talk to anyone."

"I'm sorry you're missing out on the vacation you planned, Quinn."

"It's not just that! It's also what's happened with Alan! Oh, I know he isn't a prize. It's not that he isn't good-looking or not successful, because he's both. Some of my friends have threatened to snatch him away and I know they're not teasing." Her words sent sparks of jealousy streaking through Santee's body. "But I've known him all my life and I can only see him as a brother." He suddenly felt much better. "He doesn't..." She looked off into space trying to conjure up the right description. Her shoulders rose and fell with a resigned sigh. "He doesn't make me zing."

"Zing?"

Quinn nodded, now so lost in what she was saying, she didn't notice him advancing her way. "He kisses me—I feel nothing. And it's not that he isn't a good kisser," she went on, oblivious to the dark clouds again obscuring Santee's features. "I've had friends say he can make them see double, but with me—" she shrugged "—nothing. Zip. *Nada*."

"What happens when I kiss you?" His quiet voice was meant to inspire trust.

She rolled her eyes, not realizing she was blindly walking into his trap. "With you, zing is an understatement. Buddy, you make rational thought fly right out of a woman's mind." She used her hands to punctuate her words as she spoke, still unaware he was moving closer to her. "Do you realize how potent you are?" She obviously considered her question a rhetorical one since she continued talking. "I know a lot of women are turned on by police officers, but since I've never seen you in your uniform, I can't say that's the reason, can I? So, what is it about you that makes me so crazy? What—" Her question was smothered by his mouth suddenly covering hers.

Santee's first intention was to shock her into silence. Then her lips softened under his and slightly parted for his tongue to slide inside. With each breath he took, the erotic aroma of her body lotion, along with her own personal scent, filled his senses. He wrapped his arms around her and pulled her to her feet while her arms looped around his neck at the same time.

Quinn's head spun crazily as he nibbled on her lower lip and gently pulled on it with his teeth.

"Potent, huh?" he murmured against her mouth. "That sounds pretty good to me. Along with making rational thought fly right out of your head. Let's see how far I can go with that."

"Santee, do us both a favor and shut up," she moaned, hugging him tighter against her as she arched her body against his.

The flannel of Quinn's top felt abrasive against his bare skin as he rotated his body to more easily fit against hers. With a growl of frustration, he hooked his fingers in the top and jerked it open. Buttons flew every which way as the material dropped to each side. He bent at the waist, silently urging her to lie back on the bed as he followed her down. Making sure to keep most of his weight off her, he rolled slightly to one side. He looked down at his hand splayed across her bare midriff.

"Your skin is like silk, so beautiful," he murmured, gently rubbing in a slow circular motion. Her eyes widened, then darkened to deep pools of color as the circles grew wider until his fingers ventured under her pajama bottom waistband. They lingered there for a scant second before moving on. "Touch me, Quinn."

She ran her palms along the muscled expanse of his chest. A tiny frown wrinkled her forehead as her fingertips encountered a rough circular patch of skin. She continued tracing it as she lifted her eyes in a silent question.

"Unfortunately, real-life cops sometimes have trouble escaping bullets or dodging knives."

She immediately raised her head and placed her lips against the wound. He hissed what could have been a curse or a prayer as her mouth caressed his skin.

"It was a long time ago, Quinn," he whispered with a raw sound running through his voice.

"I always liked the idea of kissing hurts better," she whispered back, continuing to nuzzle the hair-frosted skin. His skin was warm against her cheek, with a musky scent that was as comforting as it was arousing. It didn't take her long to find the slash of white from a knife wound and another round puckered scar. Each one received special attention.

Santee groaned and gathered her more fully against him. They had no idea which one pushed off his sweatpants or her pajama bottoms. As if it truly mattered by that time.

Quinn whimpered as Santee's mouth fastened on her breast, his lips drawing her distended nipple deeper into the warm wet cavern of his mouth.

"Santee," she moaned, digging her fingers into his scalp.

He pulled back a fraction and blew gently on the damp skin. He smiled when her skin quivered in reaction.

"The deep blush of a rose," he murmured before nipping the puckered skin, then curling his tongue around it. "Quinn O'Hara, you are a very beautiful woman all the way down to those red polished toes."

Her breath came out in short pants as she moved restlessly under his wandering hands and searching lips, arching up each time his fingers lingered near her feminine center. She blindly groped, finally digging her fingers into his hips and trying to pull him closer to her. He easily evaded her.

"Oh, no, I intend us to enjoy this as long as possible," he whispered, running his hand across her midriff, noticing how the skin rippled under his touch. He continued his maddening exploration by just skimming the dark curling hair and moving downward to her thighs, which slightly parted at his light touch. He dipped his head to press feathery kisses along her damp forehead and along her temples.

"I should be the one doing the seducing. Then I'd have you in my power and you'd be willing to divulge your first name," she breathed, relishing the feel of his damp skin under her hands.

"Don't worry, sweetheart, you can practice your wiles on me as much as you want." His words were barely audible as he nibbled on her lips. "I'm up for anything you have in mind."

"Yes, I can tell. *Ah!*" Her husky laughter was choked off when his fingers slipped into her velvety depths. He began a slow rotating motion that sent waves of heat flowing through her body. She arched her back, pushing the back of her head deeper into the pillow.

"Just let it happen, Quinn," Santee whispered, sensing it wouldn't take much more to send her soaring. He deliberately slowed the rhythm, feeling her contractions grip him in a loving hold.

She closed her eyes against the tidal waves buffeting her. "I want you inside me," she panted, blindly reaching for him. "I don't want to go alone. I want you with me."

He caressed the curve of her ear with his parted lips even as he continued the circular motion inside her. "Don't worry, I'll be with you, darlin'." As he spoke the words, he rubbed his thumb across the tiny nub nestled within her feminine center. As her body convulsed, he rose over her and plunged downward at the same time as his mouth captured hers and his tongue slid between her lips.

Quinn wanted to close her eyes against the lightning bolts shooting through her veins as Santee brought a whole new meaning to sexual possession. Instead, they widened as she stared upward into his eyes, dark with the same knowledge flowing within her. She bit into his shoulder, feeling his body jerk. Her damp skin slid slickly across his as their joined bodies swiftly flew upward to create another fusion that would rock them off their preconceived foundations: a fusion of the soul.

Quinn's labored breathing was the first thing she noticed. Santee had levered himself up partly on his elbows to relieve her of most of his weight as he also exerted himself to regain his breath.

"Is that—" he coughed to relieve the harshness in his voice "—is that what they call a mystical experience?'' When he rolled onto his side, he kept one arm draped across her waist, needing to maintain the physical contact.

She shook her head since she doubted her vocal chords could work just yet. She ran her fingers across his shoulder, then paused when she found the reddened indentation. She was stunned she could have done such a thing. "I guess I got a little carried away." She leaned over and kissed the teeth marks as a silent apology.

"Honey, you can get carried away any time you like." Feeling the goose bumps dot her skin, he reached down and pulled the covers up over them. He shifted her so she lay against him with her rear nestled against his groin.

"We need to talk," Quinn murmured, suddenly feeling very sleepy. She unconsciously snuggled closer to him.

"Later." He pressed a butterfly kiss against her bare shoulder.

"It's winter. I never sleep naked during the winter, it's too cold to do that." She yawned, feeling herself drift off, no matter how hard she tried to stay awake. "I need to put my pajamas on." Her mouth opened in a jaw-stretching yawn. "And socks."

"You're fine," Santee assured her, wrapping both arms around her.

"Nice. Warm." She mumbled the disjointed words into his arm where her cheek lay pillowed as she finally succumbed to sleep.

But when Santee finally fell asleep, his thoughts were centered on the memory of the sounds of her cries and the feel of her teeth in his flesh.

A GENTLE WAFT of cold air and a stirring in the atmosphere woke Santee much later. He opened his eyes, waiting for them to adjust to the dark room. He didn't need to turn over to know he was alone in the bed. He already sensed she wasn't there and felt a pang of sorrow until he saw the light shining through the slit under the closed bathroom door. He felt assured she wasn't far off and he soon could hear the snap of the light switch and the door open. A blanket-shrouded figure slipped into the room, but instead of returning to the bed, she went to the window and parted the curtain to look outside. As if seeing something that interested her, she leaned forward more, bracing her drawn-up knee on the window seat as she splayed her fingers against the glass.

"See anything interesting?" He spoke in a low voice so as not to startle her.

"It's snowing." Her voice was equally hushed as she hitched the blanket tighter around her body.

He climbed out of bed and walked over to her. He gently tugged one end of the blanket free and wrapped it around himself as he slipped his arms around her waist and pulled her against his chest to keep her warm. They watched the falling snowflakes in silence.

"Do you know what's so odd?" Quinn murmured, resting her hands on his linked hands at her waist.

"Not us, I hope."

She shook her head. "The snow is always white, even on the ground. The town roads are always cleared, even when it snows all night. And the snowfall is always—" she racked her brain for the right word "—gentle, I guess. I look out every night and it reminds me of a Currier and Ives drawing. I expect to see a horse-drawn sleigh appear at the end of the road. Or maybe Santa Claus flying across the moon." She inclined her head toward the top of the sky where a brilliant white full moon sent shafts of silvery light streaming down on the snow. "That's another thing that's so odd. I thought we were entering the quarter-moon phase, and yet we've had a full moon since we've arrived here."

"Maybe the moon is magic, too." He chuckled softly, resting his chin on the top of her head after dropping a kiss on the tousled curls. The soft fragrance of her skin filled his nostrils and reminded him again of what it felt like to have her wrapped around him.

"Along with the town?" She played along with his whimsy.

"Why not? It would make sense, wouldn't it? Didn't old Alan tell you the operator told him there was no such town," he playfully whispered, using his nose to nudge a lock of hair away from her ear. "And weren't you the one who told me that all the times you drove up this way to Crystal Falls Lodge, you never saw any indication that this town was here?''

She shrugged. ''There was no guarantee I would have noticed anything indicating its presence. I usually acted on automatic pilot that sent my car straight to the lodge.'' She turned, and circled his waist with her arms. ''Besides, do we really care if this town sprung from some kind of holiday magic spell? A holiday aphrodisiac.'' She laughed softly, tipping her head back so she could see him better. ''Maybe staying in a magical town will give us a new perspective on the world.''

Santee sat down on the wide window seat and tugged Quinn down onto his lap. He draped the blanket around them so they were wrapped in a warm cocoon of soft forest green wool. She turned her cheek so it rested against his chest while they silently watched the white flakes dance in a gentle breeze before drifting to the ground.

''Feel the glass,'' she whispered, in keeping with the awesome sight before them. She placed her hand against the window. ''It's warm.''

Santee placed his hand next to hers and was surprised to find she was right. The glass wasn't icy cold to the touch the way he expected it to be. Instead, he felt a slight warmth against his palm as if it had been stored up from warmer days to be dispensed when the weather cooled.

''Maybe it's some kind of special glass that collects the heat in the room,'' he said finally, finding it increasingly more difficult to concentrate on anything but the enticing weight of this naked woman sitting on his lap. "I never knew temptation could be so much fun." He casually adjusted his other hand to rest just beneath her breast. A soft exhalation of breath told him she wasn't immune to what was happening, either. "Turn around to face me," he said, his voice harsh with renewed desire.

Quinn slowly swung around. Her expression didn't give anything away, but the light in her eyes said more than enough.

"Slide your legs around my waist."

As she did so, her moist center brushed his erection. Santee uttered a harsh profanity that brought a smile to Quinn's lips.

"Is something bothering you?"

"Nothing that you can't handle." He grasped her at the waist and lifted her up slightly, but she tightened her knees to stop him.

"You said you'd let me practice on you, so that's what I intend to do." She undulated against him in a way that brought her eyes level with his and ignited a tiny spark of pleasure in her and a hotter one in him. She shifted her body back, each time rubbing against him just a little more. Tiny puffs of air escaped her lungs as she kept her eyes squarely focused on his. The blue in her eyes disappeared completely as the deepening gray took over. A faint sheen of perspiration dampened her upper lip.

Santee was positive every blood vessel in his body was about to burst. Each time he felt her body moistening his tip, he wanted nothing more than to grab her and place her on his straining shaft to relieve the pleasure and pain she was giving him. At the same time, her sensual teasing was making him hotter by the second and he could see she was also close to exploding, so he was determined to see it through. Even if it meant dying in the end. He gritted his teeth as she brushed against him again. As if that wasn't bad enough, she leaned forward and touched her tongue to his nipple. He was positive his chest was being flayed!

"You taste salty," she murmured against his skin. "How do I taste?"

"So sweet I can't get enough," he said between clenched teeth, rocking his hips against hers. "My God, Quinn, you're killing me!"

She trailed her fingers across his chest and downward until they touched the thicker growth of hair. When she touched him, Santee bucked as if she'd pressed a burning hot brand against him.

Quinn slowly lifted herself up and just as slowly lowered herself down. Santee hissed as she enveloped him in her heated dampness.

This time there was no rushing to the stars but a slow heated ascent. Each movement was slow, deliberate, with a pause to further heighten their sensations as they continued to watch each other, each gauging the other's reaction. The knot inside Quinn tightened to an unbearable pitch as she felt him inside her, touching areas that grew ultrasensitive with each passing second. Her entire body quivered with minute explosions beginning deep within her. She knew she couldn't keep it up much longer, just as the tension coiled within Santee's body communicated to her his control was unraveling.

Their mouths slammed together in a fusion that rivalled any atomic bomb. Frantic, needy, hungry with incredible heat. Sounds uttered deep in their throats made sense to them only as their ravenous mouths shifted for even closer contact.

Inner explosions ignited ones along her outer nerve endings. A cry tore its way out of her throat as she felt him erupt inside her at the moment that her inner sheath convulsed around him. She fell forward, burying her face against the curve of his shoulder, inhaling the warm musky fragrance of his skin, now lightly overlaid with her own scent.

"I've never..." Her voice trailed off. She moistened her lips as she shook with aftershocks still rocking her inner core.

His own arms still quivered with a reaction that unnerved him as much as it did her. He couldn't find the words to describe what had just happened, either.

Quinn half turned her head and laughed softly as she found the window frosted by the steam from their overheated bodies.

"Look what we did to the window." She used her fingertip to draw a heart on the steamed glass. "What if someone decided to take a late-night walk and walked by here? What if they happened to look up and saw us? Talk about embarrassing."

Santee held her so close against him that she could have been grafted onto his body. She felt his smile, his love. "Embarrassed, hell. Any sane person would envy us."

Chapter Ten

When Quinn woke up a second time, an unsettling thump in the pit of her stomach was already sending up warnings, loud and clear. Just how was she going to handle the "morning after" routine without looking and sounding like the amateur she knew she was? Looking down to the end of the bed and finding a very satisfied-looking Santee didn't help at all. She resisted the urge to pull the covers over her head and pretend this had been one very crazy and erotic dream. Except dreams didn't leave her feeling as if she'd just won first prize in a sex marathon!

She should have known Santee wouldn't give her a chance to regroup.

"Up and at 'em, sleepyhead." He pulled the covers down to the end of the bed.

"Augh!" When the chilly morning air hit her bare skin, she jumped up as if she'd been tossed out of the bed. "That is very cruel." She snatched up her pajama top and pulled it over her head, cringing as the cold material assaulted her bare skin.

His grin told her he thought the exact opposite. "Be good and I'll feed you breakfast."

Feeling more in command now, she sauntered past him and trailed her fingers across his jaw, which she found was moist and freshly shaven. "Honey child, you know very well I was much better than good." She kept up her hip-swinging walk as she strolled into the bathroom and flashed him a wicked smile as she slowly closed the door.

It turned out that the "morning after" etiquette turned out to be pretty painless, after all.

"PEOPLE ARE looking at us," Quinn murmured as they were seated in the dining room. She cast quick glances around and discovered that looking at the plates only reminded her just how hungry she was. "I just bet they know everything we did last night."

"You're just imagining it." Santee greeted Edna with a brilliant smile. "Hey, gorgeous, what's on the menu this morning?"

The waitress looked from one to the other and suddenly grinned. "How about I surprise you?"

Santee looked questioningly at Quinn. As she lifted her eyes to reply, the expression in his eyes dried up any words she might have spoken. He knew immediately he couldn't have said a word if his life depended on it.

"I'll come back when you return to earth." With her grin growing broader by the minute, the woman slipped away.

"You have to stop this," Quinn whispered frantically.

He bent his head to whisper in her ear, "Do you know how sexy you look when you're putting on your makeup?" His finger brushed a fiery path across the top of her hand. "When you put on your mascara, your tongue sticks out a little. Talk about tempting." His voice lowered to a husky purr.

She was positive all the oxygen had been sucked out of the room. "It's supposed . . . to relax the eye muscles." She stumbled over the words. "And, Santee, if you don't stop that, so help me, I will push you onto this table and attack you."

He held his arms out wide from his body. "Do you see me resisting?"

"I doubt you need the stimulant, but I'm sure the caffeine will come in handy." Edna plopped a filled cup down in front of each of them. She paused. "Unless you'd prefer glasses of ice water."

He shot her a telling glance. "Get lost."

Not the least upset by his brusque order, she curtsied and hurried off. "With pleasure."

"I'm surprised she didn't dump your coffee in your lap." Quinn could feel the blush burning her cheeks.

"She's a smart lady, that's all."

She started to pick up her cup but found her fingers trembling. "Let me explain something to you," she said in a low voice. "As painful as it is to admit, my experience with 'boy/girl sleepovers' isn't all that extensive."

"Not even with Alan?"

She read the tension in his voice and understood what he was really asking. "He never pushed."

The relief in his body was evident. "Not like me?"

Quinn shook her head. "He believed in analyzing every situation before taking that next step."

He whistled a soft tune under his breath.

"Here you go." Edna placed dishes in front of them and quickly exited.

Quinn stared at the plate in front of her, trying hard not to burst out laughing. "Can you believe this?"

Santee stared at his own plate, a twin to Quinn's. The heart-shaped waffle was outlined with rich swirls of whipped cream and covered in the middle with cut-up juicy red strawberries.

"I guess this is Edna's idea of a surprise," he said, picking up his fork and twirling the tines through the whipped cream.

"These strawberries are fresh, not frozen," she commented, after picking up a piece of fruit and biting into it.

He tried a piece and discovered she was right. "Magic. Remember?"

Quinn thought of what the magic had wrought the night before and blushed again.

"After last night, you can still blush?" he continued teasing lightly. "After all, you were the one to—" He leaned over and whispered the rest in her ear.

She was positive everyone could tell what he was saying to her by the stunned expression on her face. Santee leaned back and blandly cut his waffle into bite-size pieces. He forked up a piece of waffle with a strawberry piece and dipped it into the whipped cream before holding it in front of her lips.

"You better take it before people notice what I'm doing."

She slowly opened her mouth and bit down, allowing the sweet flavors to explode within.

Santee took the second piece for himself. "I wonder if I could swipe some of that whipped cream out of the kitchen without anyone noticing," he mused aloud.

Quinn's bones turned to water at the ideas his comment brought to mind. She decided it was better to tackle her food.

"Are we in a hurry?" he asked, watching her.

"The best place for you right now is outside in all that icy cold snow."

"That's what you think."

"That's what I *know*. Buster, you need to cool off that king-size libido of yours!"

"King-size?" He thought about it. "I like the sound of that."

As Quinn looked up, she froze at the sight in the hallway just outside the dining room. Alice stood before her grandmother with her head bowed, her tiny chin wobbling as if she was trying very hard not to cry.

Quinn set her fork down. Her appetite had suddenly disappeared. A faint memory of herself standing before her grandmother surfaced. One she had kept hidden for more than twenty years.

"Listen to me, young lady, it isn't my fault your parents don't have the sense the good Lord gave them. If they prefer to run around partying without bothering to buy you Christmas gifts, that's their problem, not mine. You're old enough to realize that Christmas is just another day of the year. Just as you need to realize that you'll always have to rely on yourself because they aren't going to be around for you."

"Quinn?"

She blinked several times as she slowly returned to the present. By the expression on his face, he must have spoken to her more than once.

She forced a smile to her lips. "I'm sorry, I guess I was daydreaming."

Santee obviously didn't believe her. "What's wrong?"

"Old memories," she whispered. "Nothing I'd care to talk about right now." She looked in the direction of the hallway again, but it was empty now. She had an unsettling feeling in her stomach as she slowly finished her breakfast.

"Forget it. No way."

"Chicken."

"Just call me Foghorn Leghorn," he calmly replied, referring to the cartoon rooster. Santee refused to budge from his spot on the wooden bleachers built on the edge of a large frozen pond.

Quinn bent from the waist, bringing her face close to his. "There's nothing to it, Mr. No-First-Name Santee." She deliberately enunciated each word with a coy purse of the lips.

He grinned at her obvious attempt. "You're asking my legs to do impossible things."

"After last night, I can't imagine there's anything you would consider impossible," Quinn crooned, holding her hands up, the fingers wiggling in a "come on" gesture. "All you have to do is get up." She made a kissing sound.

He leaned back against the bleacher behind him and laced his fingers behind his head, all the while wanting nothing more than to give in to his first instinct and drag her back to the inn for a lot of warm loving.

"You know, you're acting pretty cocky out here in public." He tipped his head to one side as he studied her cheeks flushed and eyes sparkling from the cold. "Why don't we go off somewhere private and see if you'll act the same way."

She moved herself in a backward glide. "I'm the one out here on the ice, not you. You've already paid the skate rental, why not come out with me? I'll make sure you don't fall down on those sexy buns of yours."

Not one to resist a challenge for long, he uncoiled himself from the bleachers and, by holding on to a short railing set alongside the edge of the pond, he made it out onto the slippery surface without embarrassing himself.

"I suppose you took lessons." He tried to look nonchalant as he held on to the railing with a death grip while his ankles kept turning inward. Even holding on, he almost slid to his knees a few times.

"For six years. My mother envisioned another Peggy Fleming or Dorothy Hamill." Quinn twisted her body, sending it into a dizzying spin before coming to an abrupt stop. "I competed twice and got mediocre scores. Then she thought I'd do better as half of a pair, but that was a disaster. I think my partner quit skating altogether not long after that." She wrinkled her nose as she skated backward with one leg bent behind her. Then, with a tiny wiggle of the hips, she cut a shallow wavy line in the ice. She held out her hands. "Come on, once you start moving you'll be fine. I'll hold on to you."

The minute Santee left the security of the railing, he could feel his ankles starting to buckle again and he rotated his arms like a windmill. Quinn got hold of him just before he lost the war with gravity. He pitched forward, latching on to her in the desperate way a drowning victim grabs on to a life preserver. Her face tensed from the strain of keeping him upright so he wouldn't drag her down with him.

"Whose brilliant idea was this?" he growled, trying vainly to listen to her instructions about ankles, knees and feet going straight and not off in two separate directions.

"Mrs. Berry's. She said after such a large breakfast, we might want to burn off the calories by ice-skating out here. It seems to be one of the town's popular pastimes."

"Remind me to arrest her when we get back to the inn." His face was twisted in a scowl as he concentrated on listening to Quinn's instructions and making sure he didn't make an ass of himself.

"Even a legal novice like me knows she's a bit out of your jurisdiction." She took quick glances over her shoulder as she skated backward while holding on to his two wrists. "Try gliding instead of taking all those tiny steps. That's right. You're doing fine."

"First time?" The young man from the movie theater sped by with a broad grin splitting his face.

"And last," he insisted.

He immediately slowed down. "No, once it's in your blood, you can't stop."

"That's right, act as if you've been skating for hundreds of years," Santee muttered.

The man laughed and skated on.

"I must have been crazy to go along with this," he grumbled, lurching forward and almost throwing them both off-balance.

"Don't look down at your feet!" she ordered. "Just watch me and you'll be all right."

His head had snapped up the moment she spoke. "Now that's something I can handle."

Santee wasn't kidding, either. He enjoyed looking at Quinn bundled up in her figure-hugging hot-pink ski pants and pink-and-turquoise parka. Her bright pink cap was tipped coyly over one eye. She looked like a little girl all bundled up to play in the snow. She looked like a woman he wouldn't mind stripping out of her clothing.

"But I *won't* hurt myself. I promise! Mommy taught me how to skate. I can do it."

Quinn spun around at the sound of the little girl's voice. Alice stood at the edge of the pond with her grandmother. Dressed in a bright red snowsuit with her dark curls brushed up away from her face in a ponytail that bounced off her neck, she brought to mind a time Quinn had had a similar snowsuit when she was a similar age.

Without a second thought, she released Santee's hands and skated over to the duo.

"I'll skate with Alice," she offered, smiling as the little girl's face lit up.

She turned to her grandmother. "Can I?"

"May I," she instantly corrected, turning to Quinn with an angry glint in her eye. "You can't stop interfering, can you?"

Quinn shouldn't have been taken aback by the older woman's open hostility, but she still hadn't expected it. "I know you and I haven't exactly been cordial toward each other since that first time, but does that mean Alice has to suffer because of it?" she said in a low voice. "There were too many times when I was her age and was told no just because my grandmother didn't want to go out of her way to do anything for me. Don't let that happen with the two of you."

Clarissa's eyes flicked downward to Alice. The little girl smiled hopefully as she gazed at her grandmother.

"You'll be careful?" she said finally.

"Oh, yes," Alice vowed with the solemn manner only a small child can display.

"Then you can go out for a little while. I'll wait for you over there." She gestured toward the bleachers.

Alice immediately dropped to the narrow bench and pulled off her boots. Within seconds she had her skates on and haphazardly laced. Quinn laughed and squatted to lace them up properly.

"We don't want you to get out there and skate right out of them, do we?" she teased, straightening up and holding out her hands.

Santee gingerly made his way over to the bench that Quinn and the little girl had just vacated and collapsed on the hard surface with a sigh of relief. He stretched his legs out in front of him and watched them glide across the icy surface. Alice's laughter rang out as Quinn twirled her. They stayed out on the ice for about fifteen minutes as Quinn held on to Alice's hand and slowly guided her through figure eights and other designs on the ice. When they returned to the bench, Alice's smile was from ear to ear, and her cheeks were rosy from the exercise.

Clarissa walked toward them and waited as Alice unlaced her skates.

"Thank you," Alice said shyly, dipping her head down as her grandmother stood behind her.

"It was nice of you to be willing to bother with a child," Clarissa said stiffly.

"I didn't consider it a bother."

Quinn watched the woman walk away with the little girl skipping at her side, chattering happily.

"Would your grandmother have allowed you to go out on the ice with a virtual stranger, even if she was watching you at all times?" Santee said, breaking into her thoughts.

At first, he thought she hadn't heard him since she hadn't answered right away.

"She resented having to look after me when my parents were gone, as it was," she replied in a low voice that throbbed with sad memories. "I was to either stay in my room and read or play with my dolls or I could go outside in the garden, as long as I didn't get my clothes dirty." She shook her head to banish the thoughts. When she turned to Santee, she was smiling. No one would have guessed she'd just been upset. She held out her hands.

"Come on, let's do some fancy skating."

"Yeah, right," he grumbled good-naturedly as he stood up, wobbling uncertainly.

Santee looked down at Quinn, seeing the forced gaiety in her manner and hoping it would fade and the real Quinn would reemerge.

Feeling his gaze on her, Quinn looked up. She was caught by the varied expressions in Santee's eyes until one took precedence. Her hands abruptly dropped from his and she skated away a short distance. The hot look was immediately replaced by panic as he flapped his arms, fighting to keep his balance. A battle he soon lost as he fell like a stone.

Quinn slid to a stop as she listened, with great awe, to Santee cursing his own stupidity, then as he moved on to damn the state of the ice and the world in general. She skated over to him and bent down with her hands on her knees.

"Hey, big boy," she mock whispered. "You're giving the kids around here quite an education with that extensive vocabulary of yours. Someone might decide you need your mouth washed out with soap."

His glare said more than enough about her gentle reprimand.

He carefully got to his feet, ignoring her outstretched hand. "There is nothing worse than a smart-mouthed woman. It's your fault I fell. If you hadn't let go of me and skated off, it wouldn't have happened."

"I figured you were ready to try it on your own. You do so well in other areas." She deliberately widened her eyes.

By taking his time, Santee made it back to the pond's edge and the security of the railing. "You go on and play Olympic skater and I'll very happily remain an observer."

"I won't let go of you again," she promised, following him with a much smoother glide than his cautious jerky steps.

He shook his head. "I'm too damn old for this, honey." He offered her a reassuring smile. "Go on. Do your thing. I'll sit over here and act in the capacity of enthusiastic audience." He sat on the bench provided for the skaters and unlaced his skates, replacing them with his boots.

After making sure he meant what he said, she pushed herself off, moving in a smooth gliding motion. He watched her effortless spins and turns with open appreciation.

"The lady seems to be enjoying herself."

Santee looked up to find Rudy, the sheriff, settling his bulk next to him.

"Quiet day?"

Rudy chuckled. "It's always quiet around here. That's why I enjoy the good job security. I guess you're not used to a town staying peaceful for so long."

He nodded. "It's a nice change of pace from rousting out drug pushers and hookers on the main drags. Say, any word of that tree being moved yet?"

Rudy shook his head. "Sorry. Since we're pretty much self-contained around here, we're listed as a low priority."

Santee frowned as other thoughts came to mind. "What if there was a medical emergency? I haven't seen an area flat enough for a helicopter to land."

"People don't get sick much in Mistletoe," he admitted. "And when they do, the doc has all the equipment necessary to handle pretty much any kind of emergency. It's a big help when bad storms hit the area and we're cut off from the outside world for more than twenty-four hours. Like what's happening now."

"I thought storms didn't hit here."

"They don't, but whatever goes on outside this valley affects us here, too." Rudy's smile was meant to reassure. "I'm just glad you folks are finding things to do. It's amazing how two perfect strangers can end up at a place where they get a chance to know each other in a way they might not have been able to otherwise."

Santee studied the older man. Normally, he'd be pretty suspicious of such glib replies. So why wasn't he automatically thinking the worst this time? He doubted it could have anything to do with a face that was so guileless it could be considered downright scary.

"Yeah, life can be pretty funny at times," he said finally. "But I'm still surprised the road crew hasn't gotten to that tree yet. I guess they can't be hurried."

Rudy grinned. "I wouldn't want to try." He grunted as he heaved himself up off the bench. "Guess I'll make my rounds. You going to the tree-lighting ceremony tonight?"

"Didn't know there was one."

"We have it every year in front of the town hall. We've got a tree there that's a couple hundred years old and takes hours and a lot of patience to decorate, but it's always worth all the trouble once the lights are turned on. Oh, I know it sounds real small-townish and old-fashioned, but it helps us remember how we're here for one another. The two of you should come."

Santee grinned at the man's automatically labeling of Quinn and him as a couple. He had to admit it had a nice sound to it. "We just might."

He watched the sheriff walk back to the parking lot, stopping every once in a while to talk to someone. He clearly knew everyone's name and paused long enough to say something personal to each one. At the same time, Santee felt a little troubled as he watched the people. Questions were lingering in the back of his mind, but he couldn't seem to bring them to the surface. It should have bothered him. So why didn't it?

"Now I KNOW why I gave up ice-skating," Quinn groaned, settling back in the hot water. She rested her head against Santee's chest

"Why?"

"Because it hurts too much afterward, when your muscles realize what you've done to them." She raised her leg, the toes pointed as she watched frothy bubbles slide down her calf. She flexed and pointed her toes several times, moaning as the aching muscles resisted each movement.

Santee sneezed as a bubble floated upward and landed under his nose. "I admit this feels good, but did you have to use bubble bath?"

"It's a very light fragrance."

"You might think so, but you're not the one people will look at funny when they get a good whiff of you," he grumbled good-naturedly as he ran the soaked sponge along her arm, slowly squeezing the water out on her skin.

She turned her head and drew in a deep breath. "You do not smell feminine, so stop complaining. If you behave, I just might wash your back."

Santee chuckled. "I'd like to see you reach my back from where you're sitting."

She waved her hand in an airy motion. "All it takes is a little shifting around." Her breath caught in her throat as he passed the sponge across her breasts. "You're having a little trouble with your sense of direction, buddy. I thought you were washing my back."

"I thought I'd start at the front and work my way around to the back." The sponge moved around her breast in a lazy circle, until it rubbed her nipple to a wonderfully painful erectness. She closed her eyes and lay back against his chest, practically purring her desire. Her arms drooped against his drawn-up thighs, which cradled her in a loving hold.

"I never realized baths could be so entertaining," he said huskily, continuing his ministrations in slow easy sweeps. The suds-filled sponge left iridescent rings of white foam around each breast before moving downward to caress her abdomen. She reflexively sucked it in. "I usually prefer showers, but I do have to say that tonight is very definitely showing me how much more comfortable bathtubs can be if you're sharing one with the right person.'' The sponge was now replaced by his fingers that tangled briefly in the tight curls at the apex of her thighs before moving downward. When her bottom undulated against his arousal, he found himself experiencing the same white-hot pleasure that he'd had the first time they'd made love. And every time after that.

Quinn's head dropped back. The cloud of her damp hair covered his face and he inhaled the subtle fragrance of her shampoo, just one of the many scents he'd already come to associate with her. He was positive each one was permanently imprinted in his memory.

How was he going to survive in the real world after this time without her turning his world upside down? He slowly inserted two fingers, massaging the unfolding petals in a gentle circular motion while his lips caressed her ear. He licked the salt from her skin.

''It's getting late. Maybe we should call down and see if they'd send our dinner upstairs,'' he whispered hoarsely as her body moved against his. ''At the rate we're going, we may not make it down there until breakfast time.''

She gulped in a deep breath of air as tiny quivers of fire moved through her. ''They don't have room service. I already checked. Just in case we needed it.''

He could feel his body tightening to the point of explosion with each touch of her skin sliding against his. He wondered if he could hang on to his sanity long enough to make this right. "Are you hungry?"

She turned around, not caring that the water sloshed over the side of the tub. With each movement, more water dripped down the side of the tub to the floor. "Yes."

His dark eyes blazed. "You want to get out and get dressed to go downstairs?"

She continued moving seductively against him. "No."

Santee arched an eyebrow at her plain unspoken meaning. "Do you want to get out and dry off?"

"What's the matter, Mr. No-Name?" she teased, easily enveloping him. "Don't tell me you never had a fantasy involving a bubble bath and a beautiful woman?"

He dug his fingertips into her rear cheeks as their bodies quickly moved in a graceful rhythm, each one's movements complementing the other's. "If I didn't before, I sure as hell have one now."

"Then why don't we work on making that fantasy come true," she whispered as their mouths merged and waves of water swept up around them.

It wasn't long before both of their fantasies were fulfilled.

Chapter Eleven

"We missed you at dinner." Mae greeted Quinn and Santee with her usual bright and bouncy smile as she came upon them. They lingered along the edge of the crowd gathered around a tree that looked to be about twenty feet high set up in the middle of the city hall's courtyard. Dressed in a bright red wool coat along with a red-and-white knit cap topping her snowy white hair and her cheeks a bright pink from the cold, she could have easily passed for the role of Mrs. Santa Claus.

"I fell asleep in the bathtub," Santee explained, then winced when Quinn unobtrusively dug her elbow into his ribs. "We grabbed a quick bite at Cupid's Café before walking over here," he continued on a whoosh of exhaled air.

"I'm just glad you two were able to attend our tree-lighting ceremony," Mae bubbled, deliberately ignoring the covert interplay between the couple. "It's a lovely ceremony and we consider it very special."

"I see old Mrs. Scrooge has decided to grace us with her presence," Quinn murmured, nodding her head toward Clarissa, who didn't look as judgmental or scornful as she usually did.

"I must say she isn't the same unhappy woman she was when she first arrived," Mae replied, as she fastidiously adjusted her bright red gloves. She looked from one to the other with eyes that looked even sharper than usual. "I think something, or someone, is causing her to do a little self-examination."

Quinn resisted the urge to fidget under the older woman's discerning gaze. She nodded as if satisfied with what she saw.

"It's a cold night, so be sure and keep her warm, dear." She patted Santee's arm as she ambled on with her spritely gait. "I would hate for her to catch a chill."

"Don't you think it's strange we've never seen her husband?" he commented in Quinn's ear as he curled an arm around her waist and drew her closer to him.

Her eyes followed the direction of his gaze. "Maybe he's another myth like Santa Claus and all those reindeer." She blew into her hands cupped around her nose to warm the chilled extremity and stamped her feet. "Is there a particular reason why we have to stand out here freezing to death while we wait for someone to plug the lights in?"

"I wanted to see what an authentic small-town Christmas tree-lighting ceremony was like. I can't imagine it would be anything like the ones out my way."

"True, Santa wearing swim trunks and arriving on a surfboard would ruin the atmosphere," Quinn said with tongue tucked firmly in cheek.

"Behave or next time I'll drown you in that bubble bath of yours," he whispered in her ear.

She thought about all the water they had to mop up after their bath because they'd gotten a little energetic. "Considering what you almost did to me the last time, I don't feel too worried."

They looked toward the tree where a podium had been set up. The man standing up there looked as if he could have been Kris and Rudy's brother.

"We wish to welcome everyone to our two hundred and forty-seventh tree lighting. Tonight our music is provided by our high school choir and orchestra," he announced to the crowd. "And as I've said for many years, the lighting of our tree is a lot easier since electricity was invented to take the place of those dangerous candles!" He finished with a laugh that swept through the crowd. He held up two large electrical plugs which he connected with a great flourish to the accompaniment of "Oh Tannenbaum."

Brilliantly colored lights began twinkling up each row of branches beginning at the bottom of the tree and illuminating the decorated branches row by row. Waves of ahs and ohs swept through the audience when the lights finished with a soft spotlight highlighting a golden haired angel set on top.

Quinn stared up at the tree, feeling what she could only describe as a sad ache deep within the pit of her stomach. She sidled closer to Santee as if needing the feel of his solid body against hers. She blinked her eyes rapidly to keep her tears contained.

"Are you all right?" he asked her, noticing how her face was scrunched in distress.

Afraid to trust her voice to speak one coherent word just then, she settled for a jerky nod of the head.

"It's so pretty." Her voice came out scratchy with unshed tears. She stared ahead with firm determination as the onlookers were invited to sing along with the choir.

Quinn looked around at the others as they sang. She saw the adults smiling, some with children snuggled warmly in their arms. The children pointed with wide-eyed awe at the magical tree as the adults watched them with loving joy. No matter how hard she racked her memory, Quinn couldn't remember a time when she'd shared moments like this with her parents or one parent and stepparent. Any Christmas split between her parents after their divorce was always spent away from home, with presents bought as an afterthought, wherever they happened to be spending the holidays that year, or she was shuttled off to her grandmother's if the adults wanted to be alone.

When she turned her head, she noticed Clarissa, her husband and Alice standing nearby. The little girl's face was bright with joy as she hopped from one foot to the other. She smiled at the teenage girls dressed as elves as they walked among the crowd cheerfully handing out candy canes to the children. Quinn didn't think twice. She walked over and touched Clarissa's arm. The older woman slowly turned her head and looked at her.

"She deserves to believe in all this," Quinn said, without even thinking of what she was saying. She didn't realize that the reason she was blinking her eyes so much was because of the tears clouding them. "When I was her age, I believed in all the magic of the holidays and because of that belief I was blind to the fact that my parents were fighting all the time. It wasn't until a few weeks later when they split up and headed for divorce court that I understood magic isn't real. That was the year I stopped believing in Santa Claus, the Tooth Fairy and the Easter Bunny. Don't let it happen to her, too. She's just too young."

Clarissa's impeccably made-up face shifted until she looked like a very tired, elderly woman. She read the silent plea in Quinn's eyes, then looked down to see the excitement shining in her granddaughter's eyes as Alice looked back up at her. Clarissa's hand trembled slightly as it hovered momentarily, then rested on the girl's shoulder.

"I love you, Gramma," Alice said, giving her a broad grin. Her attention was diverted as she craned her neck to see how close the elves were to where they were standing. She continued dancing from one foot to another in anticipation of the treat coming her way.

Clarissa looked over at Quinn. Her eyes glistened as she stared at Quinn for several long moments before turning away. For the first time, there was no icy disregard in her manner. Quinn walked away feeling as if a weight had been lifted from her heart.

"Are you all right?" Santee wrapped his arms around Quinn from behind and tugged her back against his chest. He worried about the sad expression lining her face and wished he knew what to do to erase it.

"I don't know." She choked. By dipping his head so that his ear rested against her lips, he could easily hear her barely audible words. "This isn't like me at all."

Santee smiled. He could already see the cracks in her former acid exterior. He nuzzled the candy-cane-striped cap she wore tugged down to cover her ears. A matching scarf was draped around her neck above the collar of her coat, and even her lipstick was a bright red, a more vibrant color than she normally wore. He wondered what she'd say if he told her she resembled a Christmas pixie. "Maybe it's more like the real you than you want to admit."

She shook her head, refusing to admit he might be right. But she couldn't dispute his words either. "Are you saying I might not be such a cynic after all?" Her breath warmed his ear.

"I never thought you were one, so do yourself a favor and enjoy everything that's going on. Christmas is only once a year, so we might as well make the most of it." He lifted his head and raised his voice as he joined in with the crowd's rousing rendition of "Jingle Bells."

"Around here, it seems to go on all three hundred and sixty-five days."

It was several moments before Quinn trusted her voice enough to sing along in a voice that was huskier than usual. But there was no smile on her lips for the rest of the evening. Every time Santee looked at her with concern, she deliberately kept her face turned away from him so he couldn't notice how unsettled she felt about everything—including him.

Whether it was because he could easily read her forced gaiety or because something more internal struck him, he wasn't sure. He only knew he had to reach down and wrap his hand around hers, giving it a loving squeeze. She looked up, wide-eyed. There was such an eloquent expression on her face it tore at his heart. Now he understood how easy it could be to fall in love. Because that's exactly what had happened. The cop from the West Coast had fallen in love with the advertising executive from the East Coast in a small Vermont town that believed Christmas should be celebrated three hundred and sixty-five days a year.

"Ready to go back?" he murmured. He wanted to be alone with her. He hoped he could find out what had upset her.

She nodded, and with her hand still clasped in his, she allowed him to shield her with his body as he expertly negotiated their way through the milling people.

"That was incredible." Santee spoke to break the charged silence between them as they walked back to the inn. "I've been down to Newport Harbor where the boat owners decorate their boats up with lights and have a parade in the bay. And that's sensational, but this was something for the memory books." As he talked, he noticed her distracted countenance as she glanced at darkened windows. He tugged gently on her hand. "Hey, come on back to this century."

She looked up. "Remember when we talked about feeling as if we've been cast into another world?"

He nodded. "Sure I do. So what do you think happened? That Jacob Marley's ghost got lost along the way and transported us into Christmas Past?"

Her noncommittal shrug could have been a yes or no. "Right now, it would be easy to believe. All of a sudden I'm wondering how long we've been here. And if we'll ever leave."

"That's easy. It's been . . ." He suddenly drew a blank as he tried to backtrack. His short laugh was almost embarrassed. "To be honest, I'm not all that sure. Three, four days. I think, but I won't swear to it. It could be longer, could be shorter. I'll be honest, I haven't really kept track."

"I feel as if it's been a couple days but at the same time, for all we know, we could have been here a week. Whenever we ask anyone about that fallen tree, they smile and tell us it's a low priority and to be patient. It can't take all that long to move one tree, can it?"

"Are you suggesting we're being kept prisoners in some alternate world?" he asked. "That we've been dropped into the Twilight Zone?" He started whistling the eerie music.

"Maybe we were." She sighed. "Right now, nothing would surprise me."

Santee pushed open the front door and glanced into the cozy parlor. A large silver coffee server sat on a sideboard, with china cups and plates of snacks placed alongside.

"I have to admit they don't stint on food around here. Do you want something to eat?"

"Actually, I'd prefer something hot to drink."

Quinn pulled off her boots and curled up in a love seat while Santee sat on the other end after getting them cups of coffee. She sipped her coffee, taking the time to savor the hot brew that quickly warmed her cold insides.

"Maybe I'm just suffering from Christmas overload." She was the first to break the companionable silence. "Everywhere we turn we see signs of Christmas. Admittedly, the time of year makes it appropriate, but they have this every day of the year and don't seem to mind that they can never get away from it. And they're so cheerful you almost wonder if there isn't some happy drug dropped in the water." She studied the plate set on the cushion between them and finally settled on a macaroon. "Look at this." She held up the cookie. "It's shaped like a snowman! Macaroons are supposed to be round, soft and chewy. They're not supposed to look like a snowman or a bell or Santa." She bit off the snowman's head, effectively wiping out his chocolate-glazed mouth. She wasn't sure why she felt the need to cry. "They're just supposed to be a round glob of coconut."

He'd smiled at the way she snapped off the snowman's head.

"Do you have it out of your system now?"

She polished off the snowman and selected a small yellow frosted star-shaped cake next. "Have what out of my system?" She nibbled on the cake, pleasantly surprised to discover a rich custard filling. "If we stay here much longer I'm going to have the figure of a perfect snowman," she muttered, polishing off the cake as easily as she devoured the macaroon. She vowed to start showing some restraint.

"How about I talk to Mrs. Berry when she returns and find out if there's another road out of here," Santee suggested. "I still can't imagine that was the only road in and out. Maybe their alternate road isn't as well traveled and not good for a car, but it would be a way out. There has to be a way to bring in supplies when the weather gets real bad."

She leaned forward, excitement lighting up her face. "Do you think so? I just want . . ." She waved her hands in circles as she searched for the proper words. "I want to find out if the world as we remember it is still out there. Or if there was some nuclear catastrophe and we're the only ones left. I just want—'' She sighed. "I don't know what I want."

Santee imagined he could still smell the fresh cold air that had surrounded them outside on her skin. But his reply was negated when voices were heard in the entryway.

"I guess our private time is over," he murmured. "At least until we go upstairs."

"Oh, I'm glad you two helped yourselves," Mae said when she entered the parlor with several people behind her. "I had an idea everyone would be ready for a hot drink and a snack afterwards."

"I'm going to sneak some cookies upstairs while you talk to Mae," Quinn murmured, after finishing her coffee. She smiled at the older woman as she left the room.

By the time Santee walked into his room, Quinn had undressed and was curled up in his bed reading a lurid murder mystery and munching on another star-shaped cake.

"Isn't your choice of reading material a bit out of place? Or did the author depict Santa as a serial murderer who only kills on Christmas Eve?" He flicked the book's cover as he sat down on the side of the bed next to her hip.

"Did you ask her about an alternate road?"

"She said she'd heard tonight that the road crew was supposed to move the tree off the road in the next few days. She'll let us know for sure when we come down for breakfast and she made it a point to stress the plural you when she talked to me." His mouth twitched. "I think our secret's out." He laughed as he stifled a yawn. "For someone who's used to staying up till all hours, I sure get sleepy fast lately. It must be all the clean air that gets me tired. Or maybe it's all that late night activity." His voice lowered to a husky rumble.

Quinn set her book down in her lap. She never could resist those sexy dark eyes of his. "Poor dear, you look positively worn out," she crooned, leaning forward so she could pull his sweater over his head. "I hate to think your lack of sleep is all my fault." She murmured soothingly to him as she unbuttoned his shirt and whisked it off his shoulders with crisp efficiency. "Perhaps I should consider sleeping in my own room tonight, so you can have uninterrupted rest. If that's what you want." She looked up under the cover of her eyelashes as she unbuckled his belt and whipped it out of the loops before tackling the metal tab and zipper to his jeans.

"Hey!" Laughing, he grabbed her hands. "Okay, you made your point, I don't want you to sleep in your own room."

Quinn picked up her book and tossed it across the room. "Good, because my feet have never been as warm as they are with you." She looped her arms around his neck. "I have a lot of trouble sleeping when my feet are cold."

"It is important to keep your extremities as warm as possible," he murmured, pulling her toward him.

By the time Santee recovered his wits he was duly stripped and under the covers. He still had no idea how Quinn shed her clothing without him noticing. It wasn't long before nothing else mattered other than the woman who was so enthusiastically seducing him.

"I WAS THINKING." Quinn shifted closer to Santee's body. She slowly rubbed her calf up and down his.

"No more thinking!" he moaned, keeping his eyes closed. "Your last thought almost killed me."

"Oh come on, admit it. You enjoyed every second," she purred, nuzzling the sensitive spot just behind his ear. He squirmed when the tip of her tongue darted inside his ear. He muttered unintelligibly when she blew gently on the damp skin. "Now that I have you under my power, you have to do everything I tell you to."

"I thought I was already doing that."

Her husky laughter flicked across his ultrasensitive nerve endings. He drew in several deep breaths.

"Sweetheart." She walked her fingers slowly up his chest.

He had a feeling where this was headed. "No."

"Darling," Quinn drew the word out as her lips followed her fingers.

"I'm not going to tell you."

"I haven't asked you anything yet." She touched the tip of her tongue to his nipple, then blew on it as it hardened under her patient ministrations.

"You don't have to. I already know what you're talking about and you're not getting it out of me. My first name is a closed subject."

"Is that why even your driver's license only has your initials on it." She didn't look the least bit guilty under his accusing glare. "I can't help it if it fell off the dresser and sort of opened up."

His expression was filled with disbelief. "Yeah, right."

"You have very interesting initials." This time her fingers travelled south. "They could mean a lot of things."

"Nothing you need to be interested in."

"Give me a hint."

Santee sighed. He was afraid if she kept this up, he'd give up the battle without a whimper.

"My mother was pretty whacked out from the anesthetic, okay? And my dad was feeling no pain, either. Are you happy?"

Quinn moved over on top of him. "That's not the entire story," she said, aligning her hips with his. "Give me another hint."

"That's more than enough."

"Are you afraid I'll laugh?"

"I don't have to be afraid. You will laugh and I couldn't blame you."

"What would a woman woozy on painkillers call her child?"

He grasped her hips when they began shifting a little too much in the wrong direction. He easily settled her right where he wanted her. "No more hints."

"I'll tell you about the first time a boy kissed me," she said teasingly, sliding her fingers around his arousal. He jumped under her teasing touch.

He arched an eyebrow. "Was it that memorable?"

She slowly lowered herself onto him. A soft sigh escaped her lips. "In many ways."

As she started to move, his hands stilled her. She stuck out her lower lip in an exaggerated pout. Santee's words were playful. "No way are you going to get it out of me that easily. You tell me first. Then we'll have a more in-depth discussion as we discuss both issues." His dark eyes promised her everything—and more.

She stared at him as if he'd lost his mind. She dug her nails into his waist. "You're kidding."

He shook his head. "It's making me as crazy as it's making you, so talk fast before we both fall into temptation."

"It was the summer after third grade at the girls' summer camp I attended. Danny Briscoe pulled me behind a screen in the dining hall during the boy/girl dance and planted one on me. There was only one problem with his kiss." The strain of not being able to move with the pleasurable streams moving through her body began to show on her face. The tip of her tongue appeared to caress her upper lip. He lifted his head just enough to graze her lower lip with his teeth.

It took all of Santee's self-control not to thrust upward so he could relieve the white-hot tension coiled within his gut. By then he could not have cared less what happened. How could she make matters even hotter without moving her body? How could he have been crazy enough to even start this? His voice was raw with desire. "What?"

She bent at the waist until their noses touched. "Our braces locked and we had to be taken to the infirmary where they could call a dentist in to take care of it. Danny tried to tell everyone I started the kiss, but I told him he was the dirtiest toad I ever knew and as far as I was concerned, he could drown in mud." Slowly she started to move her hips in a rotating motion.

Santee's lips twitched and his entire body started shaking with laughter. Except, all too soon, that laughter turned into something more serious. It wasn't until that last thrust inside her that he felt his soul merge with hers. When he looked into her eyes, he saw the shocked awareness he felt.

Chapter Twelve

"Is that what they call a mystical experience?" Quinn's voice was so hushed she could have been in church.

Santee pulled his pillow out from under his head and placed it over his face. He needed to think it all through before he dared say anything. Now he knew what it meant to feel drained. He felt absolutely boneless. Only Quinn's warm body stretched out alongside his reminded him he was still very much alive.

Quinn rested her face against his biceps, rubbing her cheek against the still-damp skin. Her body still trembled with the aftershocks.

"I just wish I knew why this was all happening."

He lifted a corner of the pillow. "Why is this bothering you so much?"

"Nothing's bothering me," she said too quickly. "All right, I'm bothered. Why did I speak to that woman like that? I never get involved in other people's personal lives. I know it's because of Alice. Because she reminds me of…'' She ran her tongue across her lower lip. ''She reminds me of me.''

He pushed the pillow aside. ''How?''

''How does she remind me of me?'' She managed a brief smile filled with sorrow. ''Because I went through what she's going through now. She's been packed off to a relative because Mom and/or Dad can't deal with her or don't want to. So she feels unwanted.'' Her voice lowered to a whisper. ''Unloved.''

''I don't think you were unloved, Quinn,'' he argued. ''An unloved little girl wouldn't have grown up to care enough about another little girl that she'd step in to help her.''

Quinn shook her head. ''If you think it works that way then you must have been an awfully cute little boy. And you certainly grew up to be a cute man. In looks and personality.''

''Quinn, I wasn't cute when I was a kid,'' he growled, shifting uneasily. ''I was the one with the continually blackened eye and not one redeeming quality. That's why I had teachers convinced I'd end up in the state penitentiary. And because of my acting like some damned macho kid, I ended up in more fights than the current world champ. How my mother managed to put up with all those complaints about my breaking Joe's nose or denting Greg's braces, I'll never know.''

''She saw into your future and knew you would grow up just fine,'' she murmured sleepily. ''And she was right. Look how well you turned out. You have a very important job. Instead of ending up in the state prison the way your teacher said you would, you send others there.''

He gathered her more fully into his arms and kissed her forehead. "I'm glad you can point out the good parts. Although I would hope I'd have more good qualities than just those. Maybe if we both think about it real hard, we'll come up with a few." A whispery sound alerted him to a change in the woman lying beside him. He looked down and found her sound asleep. "It seems I also put women to sleep."

"SANTEE."

"Detective."

Santee rolled over in hopes of ignoring the breathy voice that promised so much. No such luck. He opened his eyes. He had to squint against the morning glare in order to see clearly and saw a picture worth waking up to.

Quinn was kneeling over him with her tousled hair in her eyes and a sleepy pout to her lips. In deference to the morning's chilly air she wore her pajama top. He uttered a pithy epithet as he stared up at her.

"Did anyone ever tell you how rugged and dangerous you look first thing in the morning with that hint of beard?" she murmured, brushing the back of her fingers against his jawline. A faint raspy sound followed her movements.

"Not that I can recall." He chuckled, edging back a bit and sitting up. He pushed the pillows behind him as he settled back. "You fell asleep on me."

She leaned over and dropped the lightest of kisses against his mouth. Her breasts brushed against his chest as she moved in even closer. "I'm sorry I did such a horrible thing to you. Am I forgiven?"

"That depends." He grasped her hips and shifted her onto his lap.

"Depends on what?"

"On how great a morning you want to make it." The moment he touched her he knew she was ready for him. Wanted him. A soft exhalation escaped her lips as she moved her hips in the same rhythm as his knowledgeable fingers.

They moved together in a swift ballet as they rose higher than before. Quinn's eyes were tightly closed against the intense pleasure radiating through her body. She suddenly opened her eyes and watched his expression as she tightened her body around him. There was no mistaking the connection between them. She felt as if she could read his thoughts.

It's more than sex, Quinn.

I know.

I love you.

I'm afraid to say it.

Don't be.

Quinn's body shook with earthshaking tremors. She suddenly tipped her head to one side and kissed Santee with all the passion in her body. Tears dripped onto his skin as she held on to him tightly, climaxing with a force she hadn't thought possible. He quickly followed her.

Quinn's breathing was labored as she collapsed on top of him. Santee straightened out on the bed and stretched out on his side. He gathered her against him, rubbing her back in long slow strokes with his hand until the tremors started to subside. She buried her face against the curve of his neck and wrapped her arms around him.

"I love you," she murmured against his skin.

Santee's arms tightened. "Was it that hard to say?" he asked huskily.

She uttered a small laugh that throbbed with her tears. "Never lie to a cop!"

He gently ran the pad of his thumb against the delicate skin just under her eyes.

"Why are you crying?"

She shook her head. "Too much, too quickly. More than this poor brain can understand in so short a time."

He continued rubbing her back with the slow soothing strokes. He didn't want to ask her, but he had to know.

"Do you regret anything?"

When the meaning of his question registered she lifted her head. "No," she said without hesitation. "No, I don't regret any of it. Although I admit I wouldn't mind if we could take advantage of one of the hot tubs Crystal Falls Lodge has for their guests,'' she drawled.

He never felt so relieved in his life. He didn't know what he would have done if she had said yes. ''There's always the bathtub.''

Quinn shook her head. ''It's not the same. No steamy bubbling water. No way for us to sit outside under their glass enclosure where we can see the stars.''

He rolled off the bed and reached back for her. She squealed his name when he lifted her high in his arms.

''Then I guess we'll just have to put our imaginations to work, won't we?'' Santee marched off into the bathroom.

QUINN HAD THE morning to herself after Santee was cornered by Rudy who wanted to discourse, at length, about the difference in police work in a small town and a large city. She patted his shoulder as she passed him.

''Don't worry about me getting bored. I have charge cards just screaming to be used and abused.'' She blew him a kiss and walked down the street with shopping on her mind.

She stopped in front of windows, examining each display and deciding whether it was tempting her enough to go inside. She stopped by the shop she and Santee had seen the first day and eagerly studied the display with a smile that slowly disappeared. She hurried inside the shop.

The tangy scent of cinnamon mixed with the mellow aroma of vanilla teased her nostrils as she walked through. Any type of ornament that could be found on a tree she found on tables draped in either red, gold or green velvet.

She stopped at one table intrigued by the tinkling music coming from a tiny ornately decorated tree that slowly rotated.

"I've always had a fondness for music boxes."

Quinn turned around to see an elderly woman who might have come close to the five-foot mark if she stood on her toes. Her silver hair was gathered back in a knot covered by a silver net decorated with what looked like tiny rubies. A tiny pin with gold lettering announced her name was Martha. But it was her warm smile that truly caught Quinn's attention. It was as if the woman knew no strangers.

"My husband bought me my first music box on our honeymoon in Austria," she went on. "It was a lovely carved box that played a Strauss waltz. We did a great deal of traveling during the first years of our marriage and I'd always find a music box as a reminder of that particular place. Then, all I had to do was wind it up and I'd remember what we shared there."

Quinn ran her hand along the velvet cloth. "Yes, we all need special memories." She looked up. "You had an angel in your window display a few days ago."

The woman's face lit up. "Oh yes, she was so lovely that I was very tempted not to sell her."

Quinn felt her facial muscles freeze. "She's sold then?" Trying to keep them from turning down in a frown caused the muscles to quiver with the tension.

She oddly felt the urge to break down in tears and couldn't understand why. "Is there a chance you have another one?" In her mind, another wouldn't be the same, but there was something so special about the angel, she couldn't think about leaving without having even one she would consider second best.

"No, I'm sorry, she was a one of a kind. That's why I had considered not selling her," the woman explained. "She brought in a lot of customers who stayed to buy."

Quinn looked around. "I can't imagine anyone coming in here and not being tempted. I've never seen so many different kinds of ornaments." She fingered a Victorian-style gold lace fan decorated with tiny red roses.

Martha picked up a wooden ornament carved in the shape of a bell with tiny elves decorating the rim. "We always traveled during the holidays, so I was able to make many contacts and when I opened the shop, I made use of them. No one in the world has the variety I have," she proudly concluded.

Quinn wandered through the shop and found lovely items, but the angel refused to leave her mind.

"Thank you," she murmured, as she opened the front door.

"The angel brought back a special memory, didn't it?" Martha asked from behind.

Quinn's smile was sad. "Yes, I guess you could say she did." She thanked the woman again and walked outside.

Quinn's earlier joy in shopping seemed dim now as she wandered from one store window to another.

You're nuts, she accused herself. *It was one lousy angel, that's all.* Looking up and realizing a woman was looking at her with confusion, she managed a feeble smile. "Lovely day, isn't it?"

Desperate to escape before she was caught talking to herself again, Quinn disappeared into the next shop and came face-to-face with a headless mannequin.

"Oh wow," she breathed, fingering the lace sleeves of a silk kimono enveloping a matching chemise the color of candlelight. "Oh *wow*." She stared at the price tag discreetly attached to the kimono. She looked up at the clerk who had silently approached. "Is this for the set or just the kimono?"

"The kimono only," she replied.

Quinn searched and found the tag for the chemise. She blinked rapidly as black dots appeared in front of her eyes.

"I—" She coughed to clear her throat. "I have shopped pretty much all over Boston, but I can't recall seeing prices like this. This may sound tacky, but how can you sell anything in a small town like this if your prices are so high?"

"Actually, we do very well here. And there's only high prices for special items," she explained. "After all, if something is right for you, you should be willing to pay any price for it, shouldn't you?"

Quinn shook her head to clear it. "It sounds like an old proverb."

The clerk smiled. "Yes, I guess it does."

"Is there anything special I can show you?"

Quinn looked longingly at the kimono and chemise. "I think I'll just browse, thank you."

She found labels from designers all over the world and found herself picking up a bra here and a camisole there. Pretty soon her arms were filled with colorful silk and lace. She managed a smile as she laid them on the counter.

"All ready?" the clerk asked.

Quinn turned around and looked at the chemise and kimono. She mentally performed some calculations and sighed. She decided not paying for her room at Crystal Falls would save her quite a bit since she doubted the room charges here would be anywhere near as high as Crystal Falls. "I'll take those too," she told the woman. "Size small in both.

Quinn left the shop loaded down with bags and considerably poorer. She had decided she would be better off returning to the inn when the dress shop next door seemed to call her inside.

She was debating the merits of an elegant red velvet dress with an old-fashioned sweetheart neckline and a full skirt with a tight bodice when a clerk approached her.

"Would you like to try that on?"

"I'm not sure it's me," she confessed, holding the dress up against her as she studied her reflection in a mirror. "It's a very romantic-looking dress and I'm more a nineties woman."

"Romance is in the heart, not the mind." The clerk walked over to a glass case holding jewelry and pulled out a case. She returned holding a gold chain.

Quinn could immediately tell the intricate design of the chain was an art no longer practiced.

"It's lovely," she breathed, fingering the chain. Unable to resist, she held it against the dress.

"All you'd have to do is give your hair a bit more curl. Style it softer around your face," the clerk advised as she stood back.

"I know I said my charge cards were screaming to be used and abused, but I can't imagine they were thinking of this." Quinn sighed, feeling herself relenting. "But you're right. I'm going to try it on first. It may look absolutely horrible on me."

"I doubt it."

She carried the dress into the dressing room. "Unfortunately, so do I."

Quinn put on the dress and found a totally new Quinn looking back at her. She suddenly wished Santee could see her.

"Maybe I'm not such a nineties woman after all," she murmured.

"Do you need shoes to go with the dress?"

Quinn shook her head. "I have a pair of black peau de soie pumps at home that will be perfect with it." She gestured toward a rear alcove. "More dresses?"

The clerk smiled. "In a sense. Come back and look."

"I'm not sure I can afford it."

Quinn followed the clerk to the alcove.

"We're very popular for our wedding finery," the clerk explained.

Quinn couldn't stop staring at the silk-and-lace wedding gown prominently displayed. She traced the square-shaped neckline edged with tiny pearls, walked around to see the elaborate lace train and tiny pearl buttons from neckline to below the waist. Long lace-covered sleeves that ended in points at the wrist. Instead of the traditional white, the gown was the shimmering warm shade of the pearls decorating it.

"A veil or a picture hat?" she whispered.

"It's up to the wearer."

"A veil. A gown like this deserves a long veil with a seed-pearl circlet. This is the kind of wedding gown from an era when weddings took years to plan. The era when a bride traveled to Paris or London to have her gown and veil specially made," she breathed, now afraid to touch the gown for fear she'd inadvertently snag the delicate fabric. "You don't see them anymore. Not like this."

Quinn felt a burning in her eyes as she gazed at the gown. A forgotten memory made its way through the tears in the curtain holding them back.

When I grow up I want to have a beautiful wedding with lots of bridesmaids and a flower girl and lots of flowers. And I'll have an orchestra. And a big wedding cake. Everyone will be so happy that they won't want to leave my wedding because it's so pretty, a tiny Quinn had once told her mother.

Considering the family background in weddings, kiddo, I suggest you opt for eloping to Vegas. At least there, if your wedding night is a disaster you can work on your divorce the next day. Her mother laughed as if she considered it a big joke.

No it won't! I don't want to have lots of husbands like you. I'm going to have only one husband and as soon as I meet him, I'm going to marry him and he's always going to love me and I'm always going to love him. You'll see, we're going to stay married forever.

Quinn felt as if the breath had been slammed out of her chest as the words echoed in her head. Desperate to escape the memories that were crowding her mind, she spun on her heel and walked swiftly out of the shop.

"Your package! Ms. O'Hara, you forgot your package!" She was so lost in her pain, she didn't hear the clerk shouting after her.

Quinn walked until she found the shop she was looking for. She marched through it until she reached the area she was looking for. When she turned back around, she wasn't surprised to find Kris standing nearby. She looked back at the top shelf where the ballerina doll reigned. She swiped at the tears tracking her cheeks with her fingertips.

"You were right. I do need her."

Chapter Thirteen

"Quinn, are you all right?"

She thought if she was quiet he'd realize she wanted to be left alone and he'd go away. By now, she should have known better.

"Quinn, if you don't say something in the next ten seconds, I am going to assume that you drowned in the tub and I'll have to break the door down," he announced. "And as this looks like it's one of those real wood doors instead of the practically cardboard ones I'm used to kicking in, I could very well end up breaking something."

She sunk down deeper in the steaming water. "It's unlocked."

The click of the door seemed to echo in the room as Santee walked in. He shook his head at the steam filling the room and considerately closed the door to keep drafts out. He sat on the commode and regarded Quinn.

"When I came in, Mrs. Berry handed me a package that someone left for you. She said you'd forgotten it. It's in my room."

She cupped a hand and dipped it into the water, then trickled it over her knee. "Thank you."

"What's wrong, Quinn?"

"Did you enjoy your talk with the sheriff? I can't imagine they have a high crime rate here. What would they consider a major crime? Kidnapping one of Santa's elves? Or maybe taking a joyride on a reindeer."

"Any particular reason why you're in here turning yourself into a pretty good facsimile of a prune?"

She shook her head and laughed softly. "You always like to get to the heart of things, don't you? But then, I guess that's what a cop has to do. You're always on a time limit to make an arrest, so you can't make any polite chitchat."

Santee stared at her, uncertain what to make of her mood. He watched her continue to cup the water in her palm and stare at it as it trickled over her upraised knee.

"You know, I thought I'd seen you in most of your moods during these past few days. It looks like I was wrong, because this is a new one for me."

"Isn't that what makes a relationship exciting? Not knowing what's going to happen next?" Her voice was flat. She could have been talking about the weather for all the emotion she showed. Her shoulders were shaking when she lifted her hands to her head and slicked her hair away from her face.

Santee uttered a pithy curse as he stood up. He dipped his fingers in the water and discovered it rapidly cooling. "That's a good way to catch a chill." He grabbed a towel from the rack and urged her to her feet. He pulled the plug and helped her out of the tub. "Your lips are already turning blue." He wrapped the towel around her shoulders and began rubbing vigorously until her skin was pink. He used another to dry her torso and then down her legs. "How long have you been in here?"

Quinn shook her head. "I don't know. I came in here not long after I got back." She kept hold of the towel when Santee grabbed a third and used it on her hair. "You're using up all the towels."

"I'm sure Mrs. Berry wouldn't mind providing us with more if we need them." Satisfied she was dry, he led her back to her bedroom. "Where's your robe?"

"I don't have one with me, remember?"

Santee pushed aside the bags littering the top of the bed. A turquoise chemise fell out of one. He lifted an eyebrow as he glanced through the other bags.

"You did some shopping, all right."

Quinn stared right back. "The clerk was very helpful."

Santee was worried. Quinn's voice hadn't regained its vibrancy. If he thought it was possible, he'd swear she had sustained a great shock. Except what could happen in a warm and friendly town like Mistletoe to cause this?

"Come on." He rummaged through the drawers and her suitcase. "Where are your pajamas and socks?"

"I haven't needed them for the past few nights." She sat on the bed and watched him hunt through her things. "Is this how you conduct a search? No wonder you can't find anything. You need a lighter hand. Why don't you try under the pillow?"

Santee picked up her pillow, looked down and swore. He looked at the pajamas and socks with the accusing stare Quinn was positive he must use on suspects. She wouldn't have been surprised if the garments immediately confessed.

"If you had asked nicely, I would have told you where they were. But, as usual, you were high-handed, so I decided to observe your investigative skills. You didn't do too badly."

"What the hell is wrong with you?" he roared, throwing the pajamas down on the bed. That was when he saw the open box on the table by the window.

Santee wondered why he hadn't noticed it before. He'd been too engrossed in trying to figure out what was wrong. He walked over and carefully lifted the doll out of the box. He held her up. The late-afternoon light bounced off the doll's glittering crown.

"I thought you told Kris that she was meant for someone else."

Quinn pulled a long sweatshirt and underwear out of her suitcase and drew the shirt over her head. She sat back on the edge of the bed and curled her legs up under her.

"I changed my mind. I decided she would be better off with me."

He carefully replaced the doll in the box. "Because she brought back memories of the way your life was before your parents divorced?"

She flinched at his direct hit. "You remember how we both joked that maybe we were brought here for a reason? I'm beginning to think that maybe it wasn't such a wild idea, after all."

Santee grabbed a chair and turned it around, straddling the seat. "Because of the doll?"

"Because of a lot of things." She held up a hand. "Be patient with me, Santee. I've been realizing that I've blocked out a lot of things from my past. Events that a psychologist would probably say have shaped my life ever since." She started to laugh. "I'm sure that's what Alan would say. Actually, he's hinted for quite a while that my distaste for the Christmas holidays has something to do with my mother seeing a divorce attorney on December twenty-sixth while I was sent to my grandmother's." Her lips twisted. "I don't remember ever seeing her smile. Or give a hug or do anything grandmothers should do. She preferred to lecture."

He knew he was probably learning more about her than any other human being knew. "About what?"

"Oh," she said, waving a hand around in a circle, "anything from a woman's proper duties in this world to how my mother has always been a fool when it's come to men. For about the next five or six years, I was more often than not sent to her during the holidays because my mother decided it was a perfect time to get away with either a new husband or new lover. And my father wasn't about to be outdone. They both tended to head for a warmer climate, but they always made sure not to be on the same island at the same time."

He carefully got off the chair and slowly made his way over to her. "So you celebrated Christmas with your grandmother?"

Quinn shook her head. "She believed Christmas was too commercial, so there wasn't a tree, she didn't attend any parties or allow me to, and the dinner served on Christmas Day was roast beef. She went as far to the extreme as she could."

Santee didn't hesitate now. He dropped onto the bed and wrapped his arms around her.

"My ballerina doll went everywhere I did." She remained boneless in his arms as he rocked her back and forth. "Because I could tell her everything. She never told me that I talked too loud or that I shouldn't laugh with my mouth open or that those games weren't for young ladies. She just loved me the way I was." The last words came out in a bare whisper.

"The way I love you?"

She stiffened her body at his words. She looked over her shoulder. "Really?"

Santee couldn't help smiling. "Of course. Why don't you believe me?"

She turned fully in his arms. "Because you believed in the magic in this town all along and I didn't. You enjoyed seeing Santa. I could only remember meeting one who'd had a few scotches too many. You loved sledding down that hill. I was positive I'd throw up."

"But you could make angels in the snow and I couldn't," he observed, tapping the tip of her nose for emphasis.

Quinn curled up against Santee's chest, relishing the warmth of his body and the security of his arms. Instead of feeling angry and tearful as she usually did when she thought too long about her family, she felt drained.

"It seems you've kept a lot inside for a long time," he murmured, tucking a stray curl behind her ear before dropping a kiss on that same ear. "Maybe you did need the magic of this place. I guess it was a good thing you decided to drive up this way and get sidetracked."

"It was more than just that." She ran her fingertips across the back of his arm. "I don't think it would have worked if you weren't a part of it."

"Think so?"

She could hear the smile in his voice. "I'm pretty sure, because I also think we were supposed to meet on that highway and end up here."

"You're on a roll now, don't stop," he urged.

Quinn shifted her body until she was seated comfortably on his lap.

"Be patient with me, opening up like this is new to me." Still, how could she explain to him how she felt when she saw that wedding gown? How could she tell him that, for one brief second, she imagined how she would look in that gown straight out of a fairy tale. Not only imagining herself as the bride but Santee as the groom. Surprisingly, it wasn't all that scary a prospect. "I'm starting to learn a lot about myself. And I'm starting to do some wondering. After all, if there was a reason that I was brought here, there has to be a reason for you, too."

"You had to have someone to fall in love with, didn't you?"

Quinn framed his face with her hands. "We've jumped a lot of the usual steps, haven't we?"

He grabbed her finger and nibbled on it. "I guess so. I guess someone must have decided it was time for me to find the right person and settle down. And you just happened to be the lucky lady."

"Then, I guess you won't mind if I tell you that your bad-boy charm must have gotten to me, since I think the hardest thing I was going to say was that I've fallen in love with you. And I'm already worrying about the fact that we live on separate coasts and have lived different kinds of lives." Her eloquent eyes darkened with that same distress.

His dark eyes lit up at her confession. "There's nothing to worry about, Quinn. We can work out anything that comes our way. I know we can."

"That's easy for you to say." She put her hands on his face and gently shook his head. "We've been thrown into the holiday Twilight Zone without taking those things into account. We're talking about a relationship and it's rare for long-distance ones to work out."

"Quinn, you're overreacting. Remember how you said that just thinking about Alan's relentless proposals gave you heartburn? How you were popping antacids every few seconds? Is just thinking about us as a couple doing that to you?"

She thought about it for a moment. "No." There was awed wonder in her voice, then laughter. "Not a twinge, nothing." She started bouncing up and down in his lap. "Santee, I'm cured!"

"Ah, honey, if you don't want to ruin later tonight, you're going to have to calm down a little." He had to laugh with her.

Quinn deliberately overbalanced herself, which sent Santee falling backward. She remained upright, seated firmly against the juncture of his thighs.

"Now, on to a lighter subject," she murmured, pulling her sweatshirt off over her head and tossing it to the side. "Why don't you tell me about your day with the local law?"

Santee was too busy looking at Quinn's naked breasts to consider her question. She noticed the preoccupation on her lover's face and looked down. Then looked down a little farther.

"Well, I guess there's no reason we can't discuss your day later on..."

"I'VE ALWAYS LIKED young people with large appetites," Mae bubbled, first patting Quinn on the shoulder, then Santee. She stopped at the latter and whispered something in his ear. He grinned and nodded.

"What was that about?" Quinn asked the moment they were alone again.

"What?" He stirred cream into his coffee.

"You're evading me," she accused.

"I'm not evading anything."

"Yes, you are, because you never put cream in your coffee and you just did," she concluded triumphantly.

He looked at the light brown brew and swore under his breath.

"If you keep it up, you're going to ruin your surprise."

Quinn thought about ignoring his warning but thought better of it. She liked surprises too much. She finally decided it wouldn't hurt to ask.

"Am I allowed to guess what it is?"

"You can try, but I won't tell you if you get it right."

She sipped her coffee and thought about it. "How long will I have to wait?"

Santee glanced at his watch. "About an hour or so. Think you can last?" he teased.

She adopted a haughty air. "I'll try."

After dinner, Santee suggested Quinn change into warmer clothing. She looked at him warily.

"We're not going night-sledding, are we?"

"No, this is something I know you'll enjoy," he assured her as he walked her over to the stairs.

Quinn ran up the stairs and didn't waste any time adding a thermal layer under her wool pants and heavy sweater. She snatched up her wool cap and heavy coat before running back downstairs. Santee was waiting by the front door, already wearing his coat.

"So where's my surprise?" she demanded the moment she reached the bottom step.

He merely smiled and shook his head as he opened the door. "Good thing I decided not to make you suffer for an hour. I don't think you would have lasted."

Quinn walked outside and stopped short at seeing a horse-drawn sleigh parked in front of the inn. She spun around and threw herself into his arms.

"How did you manage this?"

"I asked Mae if they had anything like this and she said she was pretty sure she could conjure something up for us." He pulled her cap down around her ears. "I think she did a pretty good job, don't you?"

"A great job. A wonderful job."

Santee helped her into the sleigh and nodded to the driver.

With a tinkling of bells tied to the horse's halter, they were off.

Santee curled his arm around her shoulders and tucked her close to his side as he adjusted the heavy wool blanket over their laps. "I have it on best assurance that our driver is very discreet."

She squeezed his thigh. "Good."

The driver guided the sleigh out of town until they were gliding over an open field.

"Don't bother asking me to stop and step away to give you two privacy for your courtin'," the driver announced. "It's a mite cold out here for that, so you'll just have to be quiet about it back there."

Quinn buried her face against Santee's neck to keep her laughter from being overheard, but there was no mistaking the reason her shoulders were shaking so hard.

"You have to be quiet about it, Quinn," he whispered in her ear, his voice betraying his own mirth.

"When he said that, I got this vision of our driver freezing into a popsicle because he'd stepped away," she whispered back. "And the sleigh running off with us into the wild unknown."

They huddled together until they were able to keep their laughter under control.

Quinn shifted around until she rested contentedly against Santee's chest. She tipped her head back and looked up at the sky.

"Look at all those stars," she breathed. "They're all so bright and clear. I never see them like this at home. Probably because out here, there are no street-lights to obscure them or buildings to block them."

"There are places near my house where you can see them like that," Santee told her.

"I thought you lived in the city."

He shook his head. "No, my house is in the hills on the outskirts of town. I bought it because the area's still pretty remote. My two dogs love it. They have the run of the property, so they can chase rabbits and squirrels to their hearts' content."

Quinn thought about it. A house, dogs. All that was missing was a woman. And she already knew he'd recently broken up with someone because there could be nothing between them. But that woman must have been in his house many times.

"Who's taking care of your dogs while you're gone?"

"My parents go up to feed them and make sure everything is all right."

She tried to swallow the lump gathering in her throat. "Tell me about your house."

With that lump growing larger, Quinn listened to Santee talk about his three-bedroom house, heard him mention the greenhouse window in the kitchen and how he could sit on his patio in the evenings and appreciate the quiet or see the hawks flying overhead during the day.

Then she visualized her condo. Sterile, trendy colors and stark, modern furniture. Was that why she was gone so much? Because she had never bothered to turn it into a home, so she preferred to go anywhere just so she wouldn't have to spend time there? Was that one more thing she had preferred to separate herself from? Would she have gone on living only half a life if she hadn't met Santee? She snuggled in closer, relishing the feel of his arms around her. He felt warmer than any blanket.

"All right, you've described your house well enough, but what about a color scheme?" Did he choose it? Did a woman? She knew she couldn't ask that.

"For what?"

"For the house, silly! Color of walls, furniture, artwork, anything!" She playfully punched his arm.

"I haven't bothered with that yet."

"If the predominant colors around here weren't red and green, I'd give you a quick course on interior decorating," she told him.

"You could always do it up yourself."

"It isn't all that easy just by hearing a description. It would be easier if I saw it personally. I'd hate to suggest something that would look terrible."

"Maybe it would be easier for you if you were living out there," he said all too casually. "Seeing the house with your own eyes."

Quinn didn't miss it the second time. "Did you say *living?*"

Santee lifted her left hand and pressed his lips against the smooth leather of her gloves. "Among other things. That is if you think you could handle being married to a cop?''

Quinn felt a curious tightening in her throat. ''Marriage?'' The word came out as a squeak.

He nodded. His gaze was watchful, intent as he gauged her reaction.

''I can understand if you're worried about your job. I wouldn't be so demanding that I'd insist you give up your career for me. I've made some pretty good connections over the years. I could see what I could find out here.''

She shook her head. ''No.'' Her reply came out in a breathy rush. ''The head of the company has been talking for the last six months about opening a branch office on the West Coast. Maybe I can help him make his decision as to where.''

The moonlight was still strong enough that Santee could see the various emotions light up Quinn's eyes as she thought out loud. Her excitement bubbled over like rare champagne.

''Do you realize this is the first time marriage has been mentioned to me without my stomach bothering me? I had no idea you were such a wonder cure! I feel like a brand-new person—''

''Does this mean yes?'' he interrupted, desperate to hear that three-letter word.

Quinn's voice skidded to a stop. ''Of course it means yes!'' She threw herself at him. ''I'm going to be so selfish and not let you go.''

"Then what would you say if I suggested we get married here? Since this is where we fell in love, it seems pretty appropriate, wouldn't you say?"

She didn't dare hope. "What about your family? Won't they be disappointed?"

"Not as long as we let them throw us a party later on," he assured her. "Once they meet you, they'll understand why I wanted to sweep you off your feet."

"And you've done it beautifully." Quinn rubbed her nose against his. "There is no way I'm taking the chance of our mouths freezing together," she whispered. "I want to go back to the room, not spend the night suffering while a doctor surgically pries us apart!"

"Since the lady said yes, you want me to head back to the inn?" the driver asked. "It's startin' to get a mite colder now."

Quinn and Santee grinned at each other.

"Yes, thank you," he said before turning back to Quinn. "I wanted to give you a proposal for the memory books," he told her, hugging her body closer to him even though its shape was difficult to decipher under her bulky clothing. He suddenly wished for the privacy of his room. The slight glaze in her eyes told him she felt the same way.

"Don't you want to know the real reason I'm marrying you?" Quinn's hand edged higher up his thigh as his tried to find her breast. He loosened a couple of buttons on her coat so he could slip his hand inside.

He cupped her breast in his palm, gently rubbing her nipple erect with his thumb.

He only hoped she'd have pity on him soon as he felt her hand creep high enough on his thigh to learn he was more than ready to figure out how to make love in a sleigh without their driver figuring out what they were doing. Otherwise, there was a good chance he could embarrass himself when he climbed out of the sleigh when they arrived back at the inn.

"Why?"

She leaned over to whisper in his ear, "Because you'll have to list your full name on a marriage license, so I'll finally get to find out what it is."

"Maybe," was all he would say.

Chapter Fourteen

"You're getting married? That's wonderful!" Mae clapped her hands together. "Oh my dears, how lovely you want to be married here!" She clasped her hands against her breast. "I promise you that we will give you a wedding you will never forget. You must let me take care of everything."

The moment Quinn and Santee walked into the inn, they'd run into Mae who announced she knew something wonderful must have happened to put such a bloom in their cheeks.

"We're not thinking of anything fancy, just a simple ceremony," Quinn suggested as Santee helped her off with her coat.

Mae looked horrified. "Oh, no, that isn't right. You just leave everything to me and you two will have the wedding you both richly deserve," she vowed with such determination Quinn didn't have the heart to protest. "Don't you worry, we can discuss everything tomorrow. We've all waited so long," she said with a sigh as the couple ascended the stairs.

"Something tells me this could be the all-time production number of the year," Santee murmured.

Quinn was still in a daze from the day's events.

"At least I have the lingerie for it." She thought of the chemise and kimono she'd bought. Was it only that morning?

"Can't wait to see it." Santee frowned as something occurred to him. He turned around. He wasn't surprised to find Mae at the foot of the stairs looking up expectantly. "Mrs. Berry, with Christmas only a couple of days away, we'd prefer the smaller ceremony. We're hoping to return to our families in time for the holiday."

"Of course you are," she soothed. "As I said, leave everything to me. Would seven-thirty Christmas night be all right? Good," she went on without waiting for his answer. "And don't worry. There's so many of us who love what seems a difficult task to some."

"Come on," Quinn bubbled, holding out her hands for his. "Let Mrs. Berry perform her magic while I perform a little of my own." She led him up the stairs and down the hallway to his room.

"Are we talking really good magic?"

"The absolute best," she breathed.

One thing Quinn believed in was fulfilling a promise to the best of her ability. She did much more than her best with Santee as they celebrated their engagement.

"Are we crazy to have the ceremony here?" Santee asked once he'd caught his breath.

"And give up a magic wedding ceremony?" Quinn said sleepily, cuddling close beside him. Her breasts still tingled from the kisses and caresses he had given them during their lovemaking. "This will be unforgettable."

He slipped his arm under her neck and brought her against him where her head fitted comfortably in the hollow of his shoulder.

"I'm going to play devil's advocate for a moment, Quinn. What if we're both wrong. What if there's no real magic here?"

She turned her head and kissed his throat. "Then I guess we must have made some pretty potent magic between ourselves, wouldn't you say?" She tipped her head back so she could see him better. "Don't do what I did, Santee. I don't believe in sitting around trying to figure out why I was supposed to finally realize what was holding me back for so long or why it was supposed to happen here. I've come to the conclusion that there was a very good reason why and I don't want to lose any of that magic."

"I have an idea Mrs. Berry is going to keep us both pretty busy for the next forty-eight hours," Santee said on a wry note.

"Well, don't worry, because if she can't come up with something for you to do, I will."

"ARE YOU REALLY going to get married here?" Alice asked Quinn. The little girl had just finished her breakfast and skipped over to Quinn's table. Santee had been kidnapped by Mae the moment the couple had come downstairs.

"That's right," she said with a smile. "In fact, if you could wait a moment, I have something I'd like to give you, with your grandmother's permission." She looked up and caught Clarissa's eye. The older woman silently nodded.

Quinn hurried upstairs and quickly returned with the distinctive box. Alice's eyes rounded with wonder as she looked inside the box. She carefully touched the glittering crown.

"She's so pretty," she whispered.

"When I was your age, I had a doll just like her," Quinn explained. "I used to tell her about school and what I did that day. And I told her all my secrets because I knew she wouldn't tell them to anyone. I loved her very much and she loved me back. I'd like you to have her."

Alice suddenly put her hands behind her back. "She's too pretty for me." Her chin wobbled with tears.

"You're just as petty as she is," Quinn insisted. "Except her hair is blond and yours is dark. She wants your love, Alice. And when you grow up, you can give her to your little girl."

Alice looked up at her with strangely adult eyes. "But don't you want to give her to your little girl when you have one?"

Quinn shook her head. "She belongs with you." She placed the box in the little girl's arms.

"Why don't you take her upstairs and play," Clarissa suggested. She waited until Alice left before turning to Quinn. "So you've decided she needs your little friend more than you do?"

"Maybe with the doll as a friend to hear secrets she feels she can't tell her other friends, she'll have a better chance of discovering life. I don't want to think of her growing up not believing in magic the way I did."

Clarissa's face creased in the first genuine smile Quinn had ever seen on the older woman. She patted Quinn's hand.

"Don't worry about Alice, Quinn. She will be fine. Just as you are now."

It wasn't until after Clarissa left that Quinn started to wonder if the older woman knew more than she let on.

"Quinn, dear, would you like to go with me to the bakery to select your cake?" Mae sang out from the dining room doorway.

"Pick out a cake, choose some flowers, order champagne," Quinn murmured, smiling at Edna as she walked out. "No biggie. We should be finished in a half hour, tops."

"Do you know how many kinds of cake there are?" she later demanded of Santee. The moment she walked into the room, she collapsed backward on the bed. As she spoke, she lifted each leg and pried off her boots, tossing them to one side. She then sat up and peeled her sweater off. "And fillings? And frostings? White, yellow, chocolate, sponge. Lemon, butter rum, raspberry fillings. Sour cream, butter cream frostings. I won't even get into all the kinds of flowers. It appears the town florist has a very large greenhouse and has all these exotic flowers I've never even heard of." She unzipped her pants and raised her hips to push them down and kicked them off.

Santee had returned to the room only a few minutes before Quinn had. He settled himself in a chair with his ankle propped on his opposite knee.

"Well?" She sat up. "Aren't you going to say anything? Or are you going to just sit there like a statue?"

"For now, I think I'll sit here and enjoy the strip show," he replied, and promptly ducked when her sweater came flying at him. "You were the one who asked."

Quinn rose to her knees. The light blue shirt she had worn under her cranberry V-necked sweater covered her thighs. Santee heaved an unhappy sigh at missing the enticing view of her bare legs.

"Mrs. Berry asked if I'd like to go with her to choose a cake and flowers," she said. "I thought it wouldn't take more than a half hour, maybe an hour. I mean, how hard can it be to order a cake and some flowers?" She went on without waiting for an answer. "For a cake, it's how many tiers, do we want a bride-and-groom decoration or a floral centerpiece on top, roses or garlands, type of cake, filling and frosting. The owner of the bakery is so excited about the wedding, that the cake will be his wedding present to us. The same with the flowers." Her voice rose with each word. "The flowers that will be decorating the chapel!"

Santee sat forward. "Chapel? I was going to ask Mrs. Berry if she minded our using her parlor."

Quinn threw back her head and started to laugh. "Darling, the parlor couldn't even begin to hold everyone."

He grew very still. "Everyone?"

"Mrs. Berry invited close to fifty people this morning alone while we ran errands." She took a deep breath. "There would have been a time when I would have flat out said that the last thing we want is a big wedding and thanks, but no thanks. But I saw the excited look on Mrs. Berry's face and realized how much she was enjoying doing this for two people she really doesn't know. I couldn't say no."

He smiled and held out his arms. Quinn charged off the bed and hopped into his lap.

"We're going to be in the middle of a circus, Santee," she moaned against his chest. "There's a lady who's volunteered to sing 'Oh Promise Me.' There was even talk about the color of tablecloths and napkins!"

"Honey, I understand," he soothed. "When my sister was planning her wedding, she hunted through stores in three counties to find just the right shade of blue for the bridesmaids' dresses. My dad was never so happy as when he gave her away at the ceremony."

"Why do people get so excited about this insanity? If I had to worry about bridesmaids and color schemes and the music, I'd have a nervous breakdown," she mumbled, slipping her arms around his waist and laying her cheek against his chest. "I told Mrs. Berry forty-eight hours is too short a time to do what she wants."

"And what did she say?"

"Not to worry!"

"Then we won't." He shifted his body so he could reach into his shirt pocket. He held out a deep red velvet box and snapped it open. "This seemed like you." He took the diamond ring out of the box and slipped it on the ring finger on her left hand.

Quinn held up her hand to admire the ring. The diamond's setting was a thin gold vine twined around the stone and etched along the sides of the band. "This is so lovely," she breathed.

"It makes it official."

"I didn't need a ring to feel official, but I'm not giving it back, either!"

Not able to go very long without touching him, she put all her feelings into her kiss. It wasn't long before the kiss wasn't enough. By the time they parted, Quinn's shirt was completely unbuttoned and her bra pushed to one side while Santee's shirt was half pulled off. Quinn's fingers were tangled in the hair blanketing his chest.

"We don't have time for this," Santee announced with great regret.

"Sure we do." She touched the tip of her tongue to his nipple. She smiled as she listened to him whisper a curse when she caressed the bulge nudging her thigh. "Don't worry, I'll be gentle."

"No, I really mean we don't. Mrs. Berry cornered me when I walked in. She was talking so fast I couldn't understand everything, but she insisted we be downstairs in half an hour."

Quinn's shoulders slumped. She could feel her arousal humming through her body. She wanted to lure Santee into the bed and burrow in the warm covers for the next few hours. The last thing she wanted was to go downstairs and be polite. "No wonder so many people go to Las Vegas or Mexico to elope. It's much easier on the nerves.

"If this town really is magic, you'd think all Mrs. Berry would have to do is snap her fingers or wiggle her nose to make things appear," she murmured. "I bet that's what Santa's helper really does instead of spending the day talking to bakers and florists and arranging to use the chapel. I mentioned going shopping so I could find a suitable dress and she told me not to worry about it because it was all taken care of, too."

"You're not the only one," he told her. "It seems I'll be wearing a tuxedo. Maybe they were afraid I'd show up in a ski suit or something!"

She wrinkled her nose. "These people are so incredible. I'm afraid we could find a symphony orchestra at the chapel tomorrow night."

"Hey, don't worry, Mrs. Berry's a wonder, but she can't put together a big production in less than twenty-four hours," he reminded her. "She'll come to see that."

"I hope so. Otherwise, I'm clicking my heels three times and getting us out of here," she vowed.

It wasn't until he heard Quinn's words that Santee realized neither of them had mentioned the fallen tree recently. Mae seemed pretty certain there was no problem in their leaving tomorrow night when he'd brought it up. No wonder they both felt as if there was magic in the town.

MAYBE THIS all happened too fast, Santee thought.

What if the magic disappears when we leave Mistletoe? Quinn worried.

They had gone downstairs that evening to find themselves surprised with a combination engagement/Christmas Eve party. When Quinn found Alice curled up in a corner chair with the ballerina doll cradled in her lap, she made a quick decision and asked the little girl to be her flower girl. Alice's broad smile was all the answer she needed.

"The nice thing about being married Christmas Day is there isn't a chance I can forget our anniversary," Santee teased Quinn late that night.

"Oh, I'm sure you'd find a way if you wanted to," she said wryly.

They had wrapped themselves in a blanket and curled up together on the window seat where they could watch the snow falling to the ground.

"Mrs. Berry said you have to disappear tomorrow since it's bad luck for the groom to see the bride before the ceremony," Quinn informed him.

He rested his chin on top of her head. "At least she didn't say anything about the groom sleeping with the bride before the ceremony."

"Actually, she did mention that she thought you had a lusty look about you," she declared in a throaty voice.

She could feel his smile when she felt his lips against her temple. "And what did you say to that?"

"I told her I'd do my best to help you keep that look."

Santee turned her around in his arms and kissed her in a gentle fashion so different from his previous hungry kisses.

"Call it prewedding jitters, but we're going to make it, aren't we?" she whispered. "We haven't gone crazy because of our being thrown together here or because there's some odd chemical in the water."

To his credit, he didn't answer her right away with glib assurances. That would have bothered her more than calmed her. He tipped his head back against the window frame and closed his eyes.

"One of the things I love most about you is your willingness to question things," he said finally. "Maybe because my work requires me to do it, I now just do it naturally. My dad is one of the most logical people around, probably a lot like you. You both have your feet on the ground and intend to keep them there. My mom is the one who wouldn't let us kids lose faith in Santa Claus and the Easter Bunny before it was time. I guess I took after her more than after my dad. They met at a party, fell in love and were married three weeks later. They're still happily married, so I guess it worked for them."

"Then it seems that rushing women to the altar runs in the family." She turned her head so she could watch the snow fall. "And maybe your family's good luck with marriage will outweigh my family's bad luck with it."

"It will."

They had no idea how long they sat there not saying anything as they watched the snow drift to the ground. Soft bells rang out in the distance to herald the midnight hour.

"Merry Christmas," Santee said softly in Quinn's ear, except by then she'd fallen asleep. He gathered her up and carried her back to the bed where he curled his body around hers and soon fell asleep, too.

QUINN WORRIED that with Mae handling all the wedding details the day would drag for her. She should have known better. She had barely finished breakfast before Mae, with a wink at Santee, rushed Quinn off as she chattered away about a facial, manicure and hair appointment. And for Santee not to expect to see Quinn again until the ceremony that evening.

"What you're talking about won't take all day," Quinn protested when Mae walked her down to Mistletoe's Beauty Rest Salon. "Besides, it's Christmas day, a holiday. No one wants to work on a holiday."

"My dear, for us, every day is Christmas. But you have only one wedding day. You and Santee have become very special to us. The least we can do is give you the day you deserve. The day you've always dreamed about." Mae kissed her cheek.

"You make it sound like a primitive female ritual." Quinn was still stunned at these people's generosity.

"I guess you could say that the way we ladies of Mistletoe prepare for our weddings is one," the older woman replied, pushing open the glass door and gesturing for Quinn to enter first. "Brides are usually nervous. The day of beauty we give them keeps them relaxed."

Quinn had occasionally taken a day where she would pamper herself with a facial and manicure and hair styling, but what she was given that day was much more. After a conditioning treatment was put on her hair, she was given a full body massage that left her feeling like overcooked spaghetti. While a soothing mask was applied to her face, she was given a foot massage and pedicure. She dutifully ate the lunch they served her although she had no idea what she ate. She had no sense of time as her skin was massaged and buffed to a rosy glow, her hair conditioned, trimmed

and styled in soft curls framing her face, which was
made-up to give off that same soft rose glow.

"I told you we don't give you a chance to feel nervous," Mae said smilingly when she picked Quinn up
at the end of the day. "We have just enough time to
reach the chapel. I took your gown over there a little
while ago."

"I haven't tried it on. What if it doesn't fit?"

"It will."

Quinn shouldn't have been surprised when she
stepped into the room at the rear of the chapel and saw
the gown hanging on a hook. Two women stood
nearby talking in low voices. They turned and smiled.

"Now I know this is either a very long dream or I've
been transported to another planet that just looks like
earth," Quinn murmured, staring at the gown. The
same one she'd seen in the shop only a couple of days
ago.

"She will look so lovely in this," one of the women
told Mae as she began unbuttoning the tiny pearl buttons that began at the neckline and ended below the
waist.

Quinn hung back. "I can't possibly wear that," she
protested. "It's obviously an expensive gown. I didn't
see the price tag when I saw it in the shop, but I can
tell."

"It's purely a display model," Mae assured her as
she deftly shed Quinn of her sweater and wool pants.

Quinn should have known they'd think of everything from the skin out. The mirror was covered as she

was dressed by the three women excitedly talking around her as if she were a precious doll.

It wasn't until the veil with its pearl circlet was carefully placed on her head and adjusted that she was allowed to see herself.

As Quinn looked in the mirror, she realized now why the gown had affected her so strongly that day.

"When I get married, I'm going to have a beautiful long dress so I'll look like a princess. It's going to be the color of Mom's pearl necklace with a lot of lace and a long train. And my veil will have a pearl crown. And we'll get married at night so there has to be a lot of candles. And everybody will be so happy and cry because we're happy."

"You look very lovely."

Quinn slowly turned around. Clarissa and Alice stood just inside the room. Alice's hair was pulled back in glossy ringlets decorated with tiny red velvet bows that matched her red velvet dress and the large red bow on the white basket she carried.

"You look very pretty, Alice," she told the little girl.

She ducked her head and offered up a shy smile. "Thank you."

Clarissa stepped forward. "I'm sure you already have the 'something old, something new, something blue'—" she nodded toward the blue garter Quinn held "—but I wasn't sure if you remembered the 'something borrowed.'" She opened her hand. An antique-looking locket lay nestled in her palm.

Quinn carefully picked it up and admired the etching in the metal. "This is very kind of you," she murmured. "Thank you."

"It's almost time," someone cried out.

If Quinn was nervous, she didn't show it. She walked into the foyer with Alice walking in front of her looking calm and composed.

By the time the organist began the wedding march and Alice took the first step down the aisle, Quinn knew she was experiencing the wedding of her dreams. Candles glowed along the sides of the chapel filled with what looked like Mistletoe's entire population. But all she saw was the tall dark-haired man standing at the front. If she thought Santee was good-looking before, she learned just how devastating he looked in a tuxedo.

"You're a dream come true," he murmured, taking her hand and clasping it between his two when she reached him.

For a woman who had feared marriage for so long, Quinn's voice was steady when she repeated her vows. Her hand didn't tremble when he slipped on the gold band that carried the same design as her engagement ring and she slipped a wider band on his ring finger. And when Santee lifted her veil to kiss her, she knew this was one decision she would never regret.

"I love you very much," she whispered against his mouth.

"Good thing, because I'm never going to let you go."

Quinn and Santee learned it wasn't to end there. A reception rivaling anything in the society pages was held in the hall with champagne for the adults and punch for the children. While there wasn't a symphony orchestra, there was a band available for dancing. Which Quinn learned Santee did as well as everything else.

A little after eleven o'clock, a horse-drawn sleigh carried them back to the inn.

"I am so sorry you have to leave so late at night." Mae's eyes were soft with apology as she stood in the inn's foyer. "But you understand, don't you?"

"Yes, we do," Santee said quietly, not at all surprised to find their luggage packed except for their traveling clothes.

"We do?" Quinn wasn't as convinced. She tugged on his sleeve. "Excuse me for pointing this out, but this happens to be our wedding night."

"We'll be fine." He gathered up his clothing. "Let's get changed." He dropped a hard kiss on Quinn's mouth. "Don't worry, darlin', I'll make it up to you."

Quinn hugged Mae as Santee loaded up the car.

"Thank you for giving me back my belief in magic," she whispered in the woman's ear.

"You had it all along, dear. You just had to allow it to come forth. The two of you have a happy life."

As they drove down the road that had first brought them to Mistletoe, Quinn looked out the passenger window and idly noticed there was no sign of a tree having been removed from the road, much less one having fallen. By then, it didn't matter. What mattered was the man seated next to her. She slid across the seat to be closer to him.

"There's something we have to consider. If Mistletoe doesn't exist, our marriage outside their city limits wouldn't, either," she brought up. "Although, the chance of seeing your full name on a marriage license would be worth it."

"Then we either live in sin or get married again. I'm voting for the latter."

Quinn started to groan, then laughed. "Well, at least I've become a quick expert on cakes and flowers and decorations!" As she looked around, she suddenly felt sad. So much had happened to her here. She knew she would work very hard to keep the magic alive. "Do you think they'll let us come back sometime?"

He smiled. "I wouldn't be surprised."

Quinn had to kiss him. "You know what? Neither would I."

Chapter Fifteen

December 26, Midnight

The ending was as silent and eloquent as the beginning.

As if guided by a master switch, the singing voices heard in the midst of the brightly lit village slowly faded until finally all was silent. After the silence, all the town's streetlamps dimmed to a faint yellow haze in the clear night air and soon disappeared altogether.

Next, as if another master switch had been thrown by an unseen hand, all the buildings began to shimmer as if a silk scarf had been placed across the camera lens recording the moment. They shimmered and gradually faded to nothingness.

A lone rabbit hunched near the stand of trees with his front paws raised upward and nose quivering in search of a scent that was no longer there.

The meadow was quiet and empty once more.

Epilogue

December 12
Vermont

"At least we don't have to worry about a blizzard this time." Quinn huddled in her down parka. "I can't believe I'm so cold!" she suddenly wailed. "All that California warmth has thinned my blood."

"We've only got a few more miles," Santee assured her.

Quinn looked at the gold band on his third finger, left hand, that matched her own. There were days when she found it incredible that this man was all hers. Funny, she never felt possessive about anyone until Santee.

She was as possessive of him as he was of his first name. She doubted if he'd want to name their first son after himself—Christopher Robin Santee. She didn't know why he was so defensive. It was a much nicer name than, say, Piglet.

In the beginning, Quinn's helping to set up her agency's West Coast office had kept her so busy she saw little of her new husband, but that had soon calmed down and they felt themselves settling into married life. When Santee surprised her at the last minute with plane tickets East and the announcement they were going back to Mistletoe, she was stunned at the very least.

"Are you sure we'll find it?" she asked softly, feeling one of many doubts she'd had lately. "When I researched the legend of the town, it said that it's only there for people who need to find a special part of themselves. And we accomplished that last year."

"It will be there," he said confidently as he turned down the side road they'd traveled a year ago. "I feel it."

"And you promised we'd be back home in time for Christmas," she reminded him, thinking of the golden-haired angel she'd placed on top of their tree. The one Santee had surprised her with on their wedding night after they had stopped at a hotel a few hours down the road.

"More than enough time."

Quinn thought of the Christmas gift she had for Santee and wondered how he was going to react to the news he was going to be a father next spring. A surprise baby thanks to a night filled with champagne and laughter, but she already knew the child would be welcomed and loved.

Santee slowed the car at the top of the rise. "Look."

In response to his hushed voice, she followed his gaze. The lights were soft in the distance and the welcoming warmth already reached out to them.

"It's there." She blinked her eyes to keep back her tears of joy.

Santee drove a little faster until they reached the edge of the town and soon, the Mistletoe Inn. They had barely climbed out of the car when the front door opened.

"Hello there!" Mae greeted them with her usual good cheer. "Come in out of the cold." She urged them inside and turned to hug Quinn. "I see marriage agrees with you."

Quinn smiled and nodded, so warmed by this wonderful woman.

Mae beamed. "I know it does, just as I know the two of you will have beautiful children beginning with the one you now carry. And it shows you have found what you both needed."

Quinn looked past her shoulder at Santee who was talking to Hollis.

"Yes, we did. And I'm glad we were allowed to come back to tell you so and to thank you," she said softly.

"Don't thank me. I'm just pleased it all worked out." Mae urged Quinn into the dining room. "Now how about some food? I personally baked some of your favorite little cakes just for you." She gestured over her shoulder for Santee to follow them.

Quinn's eyes sought his. His smile warmed her as it always did. "I won't even ask how you knew we were coming. I'm just going to relax and enjoy the Christmas magic you're giving us."

Santee walked up to her and wrapped his arms around her. "So was this a good Christmas present?" he whispered in her ear.

She looked up and smiled. "The best I could ever have."

Take 4 bestselling love stories FREE

Plus get a FREE surprise gift!

THE BABY IS ADORABLE...
BUT WHICH MAN IS HIS DADDY?

Too Many DADS

Alec Roman: He found baby Andy in a heart-shaped Valentine basket—but were finders necessarily keepers?

Jack Rourke: During his personal research into Amish culture, he got close to an Amish beauty—so close he thought he was the father.

Grady Noland: The tiny bundle of joy softened this rogue cop—and made him want to own up to what he thought were his responsibilities.

Cathy Gillen Thacker brings you TOO MANY DADS, a three-book series that asks the all-important question: Which man is about to become a daddy?

Meet the potential fathers in:
#521 BABY ON THE DOORSTEP
   February 1994
#526 DADDY TO THE RESCUE
   March 1994
#529 TOO MANY MOMS
   April 1994

DADS

'Tis the Season

...for family gatherings and holiday parties. This month's authors have put together some of their favorite recipes for Christmas dinner. Start with a *Hot Broccoli Dip*. Then serve *Standing Rib Roast* and *Copper Pennies*. Top this off with *No-Fuss, All-Sin Chocolate Truffles!*

Linda Randall Wisdom's Hot Broccoli Dip

1 to 1 1/2 lb round sourdough bread loaf
1/2 cup finely chopped celery
1/2 cup chopped red pepper
1/4 cup finely chopped onion
2 tbsp margarine
1 lb cheese spread, cubed
1 10-oz pkg frozen chopped broccoli, thawed
& drained
1/4 tsp dried rosemary leaves, crushed
assorted vegetables, for dipping

Slice top from bread loaf; remove center from bread, leaving 1-inch shell. Cut removed bread into bite-size pieces and re-cover shell with top. Place pieces and shell on cookie sheet and bake at 350° F for 15 minutes or until hot. Sauté celery, peppers and onions in margarine. Reduce heat. Add cheese spread and stir until melted. Stir in remaining ingredients; heat thoroughly, stirring constantly. Spoon into bread loaf. Serve hot with toasted bread pieces and vegetable dippers.

For the remaining three recipes, see the other December American Romances. Happy Holidays!